THE TROUBADOUR OUTLAW

JASON LEMOINE

Oeste Way Press

This is a work of fiction. Names, characters, places, and incidents either are products of the author's imagination or are used fictitiously. Any resemblance to actual persons, living or dead, or actual events is entirely coincidental.

Book Cover by Jason LeMoine

Print ISBN-13: 979-8-9947772-0-6

First printing 2026

PROLOGUE

New Mexico Territory – 1883

The cantina door creaked open, and the hum of talk fell to a hush. Mesilla was a small town, but its cantina was never empty—not with drifters, ranch hands, and wagoners moving between Tucson and El Paso. That night the air hung heavy with cigar smoke, sweat, and the sharp tang of tequila.

A tall man stepped inside. His hat was pulled low, his shirt stained with dust, and across his back hung a guitar with a scar running across its body. A revolver rode his hip, the holster smooth from use. The spurs on his boots sang against the wooden floor as he walked past the other patrons.

Someone near the bar muttered, "*Oye. El Mariachi Bandolero.*"

The man with the guitar moved with the ease of someone who'd been watched his whole life—confident but cautious. He set the guitar on a chair, tapped the counter, and said in his low, steady voice, "Whiskey."

From a table in the corner came a shout. "Play us a song, mariachi!" Miners from Santa Rita, drunk and loud. One slapped his hand on the table for emphasis.

Reluctantly, the man picked up the guitar and strummed a few chords. His fingers were calloused from strings and steel alike. The music came soft at first, then carried through the cantina like wind through canyon stone. He sang in Spanish—his voice warm and sorrowful—about a man who carried both wine and bullets, who loved women as much as he loved danger, and who knew one day the desert would take him.

The crowd hushed, listening. Even the marshal, seated near the doorway, looked up from his beer. The lawman was a thick-shouldered *mestizo* with a trimmed mustache and the weariness of a man who had buried too many.

When the song ended, the miners clapped. Their coins ringing on the table. The man with the guitar bowed his head, set the guitar back down, and turned his attention back to the bar.

The bartender poured him a shot. She was a plump, middle-aged widow with large round eyes that missed very little. She set the glass down—hard enough that the whiskey jumped. "You always bring trouble with you."

He smiled faintly, lifting the glass. "And you always save me a drink."

The lawman rose from his chair and stood next to him at the bar. "One day you'll have to choose," the marshal said.

"Between what?" he asked.

"Between the song and the gun. You can't carry both forever."

The man's smile didn't reach his eyes. "Maybe the song keeps the gun quiet."

The marshal shook his head. "Or maybe it just makes you forget what the gun's done."

Their eyes met for a long moment, neither yielding. At last, the town marshal tipped his hat and walked out into the night, boots crunching on gravel.

The bartender leaned across the counter, her voice hushed. "You ought to listen to him. Men talk about you. Some say you killed a rancher over in Ruidoso last spring. Some say you ride with bandits."

"And what do you say?" he asked, never looking up from the glass in his hand.

"I say you've got a good heart, but a man can lose it in this country faster than a coin at the tables."

He swallowed the last of the whiskey and set the glass down gently. "Then let's hope I've still got enough heart to sing tomorrow."

He placed a couple coins on the bar, slung the guitar back over his shoulder, and stepped out into the desert night. The plaza in Mesilla was lit by lanterns, shadows stretching long across adobe walls. Horses stamped and snorted at the hitching post, restless under the rising moon.

He mounted his horse and looked back at the cantina door. He could still hear the murmur of voices, laughter, the scrape of chairs. It was the sound of a world that wanted him but didn't trust him.

He rode north out of Mesilla, spurs jingling, dust rising beneath the hooves. It was a clear night. The light of the moon made it easy to navigate. The desert stretched wide and endless, black and empty under the stars. The guitar pressed against his back as he rode. In the silence of the desert, he hummed a tune—half song, half prayer.

A song for the dead and for the living. A song for himself. Because deep down, he knew the marshal was right. He would have to choose one day. He just prayed the desert would let him decide when.

1

Arizona/New Mexico Territory – 1876

Loren Ardoin was nineteen when he first heard the desert wind sing. He had been born on the banks of the Atchafalaya River in Louisiana, where the air smelled of moss and magnolia and his mother's voice carried him through every storm. His father had been a riverboat pilot, gone more often than not, leaving Loren with a fiddle and the memory of a man's laugh that echoed down wooden docks.

After the war ended in '65, Louisiana turned sour. Loren's older brother never came home from Shiloh, and his mother faded with grief. By the age of eighteen, Loren had nothing left but a worn guitar and the territories out West were calling his name.

He traded his last mule for a train ticket, played strings in railyards for food, and drifted until the rails stopped. Before long he was stepping off the platform in Las Cruces—a rawboned town stinking of sweat and ambition.

The West was no place for dreamers. The desert stripped a man down to what he truly was. Loren found that out early on when he nearly got himself killed outside a cantina called La Rosa Negra. And so he kept moving—no plan, no meaningful connection—just drifting from one town to another like a tumbleweed bounces across the open land.

He eventually tumbled into the town of Nogales. It was in this rowdy locale where his roots would finally grab into the desert earth. He'd played a set for a crowd of miners and cowhands, strumming soft ballads in Spanish though his tongue still bent toward Cajun. The coins had been few, and the men meaner than he expected.

One miner threw a bottle toward the corner where Loren was sitting and words were exchanged. A pair of vaqueros tried to drag him outside for sport. Loren had fought back and broke free of their drunken grasp. In defense, he swung his guitar like a club and connected with the shoulder of one of the men. They tumbled a bit but quickly recovered and started to draw their guns. It would've ended ugly if not for the intervention of strangers.

Five men had been seated at a table nearby watching the action unfold. The fisticuffs provided some entertainment on an otherwise uneventful night. But when the two men reached for their holsters, they all stood up and quickly approached the corner. The strangers knew the young singer was already at a disadvantage going up against the two men—even if drunk. They weren't about to allow the men to pull iron as well.

"Hey, quit messin' with the kid!" one of the strangers commanded.

One of the men snarled back, "Stay out of it or you'll be next," and then turned to see who it was that spoke. He paused and tapped his companion on the shoulder. The vaqueros quickly realized they were outnumbered. They reholstered their guns and backed away. Realizing they would not win this fight now, they retreated out the door and into the night.

Four of the strangers returned to their table—and their drinks. The man who spoke remained.

"*Gracias*," Loren said.

"Come, have a drink," the man said as he motioned toward the table where the others were seated. Loren grabbed his bag and followed to the table, then took a seat. He felt a bit uneasy—a boy, barely able to grow a mustache, among hardened men.

Introductions followed.

The leader was Mateo Vargas—stocky, broad-chested, carrying himself like a man with more burdens than he ever spoke aloud. He looked slow, but he swung a Bowie knife with terrifying ease and planned robberies with equal precision. Loud laugh. Big heart. Everyone he met was an *amigo*.

Across from him sat John Edwards. Short. Lean. Loren already heard Mateo call him "Juanito." He was impeccably dressed in a dark suit and polished boots. A Navy revolver rode each hip. His hat brim shadowed sharp, watchful eyes. Loren didn't need telling—the man was a gunfighter.

The muscle was Seamus "Red" Moran, an Irish drifter with a gambler's grin and a beard that swallowed half his face. He still dressed like the ranch hand he once was—cattleman's hat, open-collar plaid shirt, worn dungarees, and boots scarred by years of hard miles.

Beside John sat Samuel Cobb—a Kansas farm boy turned bitter. His clothes were as worn as his patience. Quick with an insult. Quicker to a fight. He drifted in and out of the gang chasing "opportunity," but trouble always sent him back again.

Finally, there was Nitis, silent as the desert night. Loose white shirt. Baggy cotton pants tucked into moccasin boots. A red headband kept his long black-and-silver hair in place. Loren had been fortunate to never come across an Apache while meandering across the territory. The sight of one sitting across the table from him was intimidating. Nitis said nothing, only watching with an unreadable stare that made Loren's stomach tighten.

At some point that night, Loren realized they had a name for themselves—*the Rubies*. They spoke to each other like brothers—easy, familiar—and Loren began to suspect they were closer than simple partners. More like a family, though none shared blood. They didn't talk like hardened outlaws. More like men who did what they had to in a land that didn't give much back.

That night outside the cantina, Mateo had clapped Loren on the back. "You got guts, *muchacho*. And music. Both are useful to men like us." Loren was invited to ride with them, and he accepted.

Their hideout was located between Nogales and Tucson near the village of Tubac. It was an old Spanish mission half swallowed by sand, its churchyard overrun with mesquite trees. The cracked bell still hung in the tower. Crows nested in the rafters.

It was there that Loren found his second family. They laughed, drank, and gambled under the moonlight. Loren would play guitar and sing ballads—songs of saints and sinners. His voice soft and melancholic.

"Your music makes us human again," Mateo told him once, drunk on mezcal. "Don't forget that. Guns make us animals. Songs... they remind us why we live, why we fight."

It did not take long, however, for the Rubies to see that Loren was no gunfighter. John took it upon himself to try.

One dusky evening at the mission, after a few of the others had gone to dice and drink, he called Loren into the yard and handed a Colt Navy to Loren. A row of glass bottles perched on a short wall.

"You got music in your hands," John said, "but music doesn't stop bullets. Let's see if you can make lead sing too."

Loren fumbled with the weapon, nearly dropping it. John's lip twitched at the clumsiness but he said nothing cruel, only adjusted Loren's grip.

"Not too tight. A gun ain't a shovel—it's an extension of your hand. Hold it like you'd hold a woman's waist."

Loren swallowed hard. "And then what?"

"Then you breathe. Aim with the breath, squeeze with the calm." John demonstrated, his arm steady as a board. He fired—the first bottle shattered into dust.

Loren lifted his revolver. The weight pulled strange in his palm, heavier than any instrument. He sighted down the barrel, drew a shaky breath, and squeezed. The shot went wide, sending a puff of dust into the churchyard wall.

Cobb laughed from where he was leaning in the doorway, but John silenced him with a glare sharp enough to cut.

"Again," John said.

For the next hour Loren fired and reloaded, missing more than he hit. John never raised his voice.

He adjusted stances, shifted shoulders, tapped Loren's wrist when it bent wrong. Finally, on the last cylinder, Loren's shot rang true—a bottle exploded in a rain of green shards.

Loren blinked, hardly believing it.

John allowed the faintest of smiles. "Not bad, *muchacho*. Someday, maybe you'll shoot near as pretty as you play."

Before long, it seemed whenever Loren had a free moment, he was back in the churchyard with John, the guitar and the pistol vying for space in his hands. One gave him music, the other survival. He didn't know which would shape him more—the strings or the steel.

***

It was early in the morning, the Rubies were riding home after a raucous night of drinking at the saloon in Tubac, when they came upon a herd of mustangs grazing near a dry wash. Mateo looked back at Loren who was riding with him. "It's time you got your own ride."

They came to a stop a distance away from the herd. Loren climbed down and grabbed a lasso off Mateo's saddle. Nitis pulled up next to Loren and dismounted.

He handed his reins to Mateo and turned to Loren, "I will come with you, *shik'isn*."

Together they slowly approached one of the mustangs that was separated from the main group. Nitis motioned for Loren to lasso the horse. Loren circled the lariat over his head a few times and then released. The loop landed around the mustang's neck. Nitis patted Loren's shoulder and motioned to proceed slowly toward the horse. "Shhh," he whispered as they got closer.

Loren held out his hand and patted the animal's strong, thick neck. Softly he said, "There, boy. I got you." Loren slowly moved to the side of the horse. The mustang sidestepped away from its captor and snorted. Nitis—still standing near the head—held up his hands to calm the steed. Loren held the rope firm and once again calmly approached. This time the horse remained still. Sensing the moment was right, Loren looked over at Nitis for approval, who nodded his head.

Loren mounted onto the horse. The mustang shifted under him, hooves crunching against the gravel of the wash. Its hide gleamed the color of pale sand, like the desert itself had lent him a creature born from sun and dust. Loren patted the horse's neck, feeling the solid muscle beneath the hide. The horse pulled a little, its nerves on edge.

Nitis took a few cautious steps back—hands still up in the air. The stoic look on his face, for a brief moment, reflected a sense of pride and satisfaction.

"Easy there, boy," Loren murmured, voice low and steady. The animal flicked an ear but didn't shy. Together—with Nitis at their side—they trotted toward the other Rubies.

Mateo let out a soft chuckle. "That horse looks near as stubborn as you, *hermano*. You gonna give him a name, or just call him *caballo* forever?"

Loren studied the horizon, where the wind pushed heat waves across the desert floor. A word came to him, soft but certain, like it had been waiting all along.

"Solano," he said. "Like the sun and the wind together."

The mustang whinnied as if in approval, and Loren allowed himself the smallest of grins. "Yeah," he whispered, stroking the mane, "you'll carry me where I need to go."

In the months that followed that introductory night in the cantina, the Rubies committed petty crimes across the desert on both sides of the border—wagon heists, small robberies, shoplifting—but nothing that caused considerable harm on the victims or attracted considerable attention from the law. They took only what they required to continue living carefree from one day to the next. Loren did not have to do much but help keep the victims calm. He would often strum a few chords on his guitar—keeping an eye out for trouble—while the others grabbed the coins, handbags, and goods.

That all changed on a cold wintry day.

2

Arizona Territory – 1876

The Rubies had been away from their mission home for weeks—bedrolls laid out each night beneath a blanket of stars, saddlebags doubling as pillows. Nitis had long ago adopted the role of cook. He hunted small game, foraged wild seeds, and gathered prickly pear and saguaro fruit. Loren had come to realize how much they depended on Nitis. The man could keep them fed for weeks without ever riding into town.

"Nitis, what have we got to eat this morning?" Red asked as he cinched his saddle.

Loren was gently brushing Solano's coat smooth. "Yeah, I'm starving. That biscuit last night wasn't enough."

Nitis reached into one of his saddlebags. "I only have a few strips of jerky."

Mateo approached. If he was concerned about the lack of food, he did not show it. His steps were light—his grin easy. "Eat what we got, *muchachos*. We'll get more." He waved them on and turned toward his horse. Nothing more needed to be said. They needed provisions and they trusted Mateo had a plan to get them. He always spoke like food, bullets, and luck would simply appear when needed. And somehow, they often did.

Once the horses were made ready, they rode toward the nearest town. Red nudged his horse closer to Loren as they rode. "Ever tell you about the time Mateo and me tried to run a freight business?"

Mateo groaned. "Don't."

"Oh, I'm tellin' it," Red said, already grinning. "Years back—before the Rubies—we decided we were done with ranching and stubborn animals. Done with law trouble too. No fights, no guns. Gonna live clean. Respectable."

"Lasted three weeks," John muttered.

"Three and a half," Red corrected. "We bought two mules off a miner in Bisbee. Fine animals. Strong. Only problem was"—he paused, dramatic—"they hated each other more than Mateo hates bad whiskey."

Mateo's mouth twitched, but he didn't argue.

"We start haulin' freight between Bisbee and Benson—coffee, flour, tools, fancy pillows. Domestic stuff. We're respectable citizens, see?" Red waved a hand. "Then one day we take a load of mirrors to Benson. Fancy eastern glass. Worth a fortune."

"What went wrong?" Loren asked.

"Well," Red said, "turns out mules don't understand reflections. Wagon hits a rut, tarp slips back, and those two bastards catch sight of themselves in the mirrors." He slapped his leg, laughing. "Them mules spooked themselves. They thought there were *four* of 'em. Started brayin' and kickin' like the world was endin'. Mateo's cussin', I'm tryin' to calm 'em, and next thing you know we've got a fortune in mirrors shatterin' across the Arizona dirt."

Nitis chuckled softly. Even John's lips twitched.

"And the merchant?" Loren asked.

"Oh, he was calm about it," Red said. "Calm as a preacher on Sunday."

Mateo sighed. "He tried to shoot us."

"Three times!" Red added proudly. "We took that as a sign from the Almighty that we weren't meant for honest work."

The laughter faded slowly. The creak of leather filled the silence. For a moment, Loren could almost forget what they were—they sounded like boys on an adventure.

Sonoita was no more than a wide, dusty crossroads where ranchers from the Santa Cruz Valley came to barter beef, hides, and horses. Freight wagons rattled through on their way between Tucson and Fort Crittenden. The Southern Pacific rails weren't here yet—just long roads and longer gossip.

The single sunblasted road that cut through town was lined with a few weathered adobe homes, a saloon with squeaky batwing doors, and the general store—the only place within thirty miles where a man could buy flour, calico, or a new Winchester if he had the coin.

The Rubies rode in at dawn, the sun still a red smear on the horizon. Loren's mustang, Solano, tossed his head at the smell of woodsmoke and horses. Loren stroked his mane to quiet his horse and calm his nerves.

A dog slept beside a trough. A girl skipped rope in the dust. A woman swept her stoop, pausing to nod politely as they passed. People went about their busi-ness—dusting, watering horses—like nothing bad ever happened here. It struck Loren that people here be-haved like the world was decent and orderly, like bad men only lived in dime novels. He wondered how long before they hated him.

"Just a quick job," Mateo said, his voice calm but firm. "We take what we need, scare the shopkeeper if he won't hand it over, and ride out before anyone knows better."

Cobb spat a stream of tobacco into the dust. "Hell with scarin'.... Man's bound to have a shotgun under that counter. I'll handle it."

Mateo gave him a hard look. "No killing unless there's no choice. We're thieves, not butchers." Cobb only grinned, which unsettled Loren more than any-thing.

The bell above the general store door jingled as they entered. The place smelled of coffee grounds, kerosene, and rawhide. Shelves sagged with sacks of flour, tins of tobacco, spools of thread.

The shopkeeper, a middle-aged man with sleeves rolled up, looked up from his ledger. His eyes flicked from Mateo's broad frame to Cobb's hard glare, then to the gun belts they made no effort to hide.

"Mornin', gentlemen," he said, voice tight. "What can I do for you?"

Red picked an apple from the stack of crates in the middle of the shop and polished it against his shirtsleeve. Loren walked over to the shelf of tonics and fingered at the various bottles. Mateo stepped forward, his tone almost cheerful.

"Fill us a sack with coin, cartridges, and whatever jerky you've got. Nice and easy."

The man's hand twitched toward the counter, where a shotgun rested just out of sight. Cobb moved faster. He drew and fired, the crack of his revolver deafening in the small room. The shopkeeper jerked back, crashing into a shelf of tin pans, blood blooming across his chest. Loren froze, the sound ringing in his ears. His stomach turned.

"Damn it, Cobb!" Mateo roared. "I said no killing!"

The two men glanced at each other. Loren anxiously searched each of their eyes. "He was reachin'!" Cobb shouted back. "Would've blown your guts out if I hadn't."

"You're always so quick to insult… and even faster to fight," John bluntly stated.

"Is that so?" Cobb, suddenly flush in the face, stared intently at John.

Their argument lasted only a heartbeat, though, as the townsfolk were reacting to the sound of the gunfire. Men poured out from the saloon, revolvers in hand. A rancher with a gray beard shouted, "Thieves! Stop 'em!"

Bullets smashed through the store windows. Glass rained down. Cobb cursed, firing wildly into the street.

"Loren!" Mateo barked. "Cover the back!"

Loren stumbled toward the rear door, heart hammering. A figure appeared—a young ranch hand with a rifle. His eyes widened as he observed the scene in front of him. For an instant they stared at each other—two boys caught in a moment. Then the rifle rose.

Loren fired first.

The recoil jolted his arm. The ranch hand staggered, a look of surprise frozen on his face, before crumpling into the dirt. Loren's stomach lurched. He wanted to run to the boy, to undo it, but Cobb's shout dragged him back. "Move, damn you!"

They burst through the back, saddling up as more shots cracked around them. Solano reared but Loren steadied him, mounting with shaking hands. Mateo led them out of town, bullets snapping at their heels, townsfolk shouting curses into the morning air.

By nightfall, they made camp in the shadow of the Santa Rita Mountains, where the Madera Canyon wound like a green ribbon through the dry hills. Soldiers from Fort Crittenden sometimes rode this country, and Apaches passed through when the season turned—but tonight, only the sycamore-lined creek spoke. The sound of water eased something tight inside Loren.

A small fire crackled. Cobb laughed, retelling the story of the shopkeeper's "surprised face," but no one joined him. Red kept his gaze on the flames, jaw tight. John sat apart, cleaning his pistols with slow, deliberate strokes. Loren sat with his back against a boulder, Solano grazing nearby. The young troubadour's hands still shook. He could see the ranch hand's eyes in the firelight—the shock of the moment burned into him.

Mateo came over, squatting beside him. His voice was low, almost fatherly.

"You did what you had to, *muchacho*. Better him than you."

Loren swallowed hard. "He couldn't have been much older than me."

Mateo laid a heavy hand on his shoulder. "This land don't care how old you are. Either you survive, or you feed the buzzards. Don't forget it." He left Loren with the creek's quiet murmur and the weight of his first kill.

Above them, the stars burned cold and far away, as if they had nothing to do with any of it. Loren strummed a single, hollow note on his guitar before setting it aside. Tonight, no song could wash away the blood.

"First one's always the loudest," Red said gently. "After that... they get quieter."

"Do they?" Loren asked. Red didn't answer.

The gang rode west in the morning. "What happened yesterday... changes things," Mateo uttered. Red nodded. John shot a glance over at Cobb, who simply shrugged his shoulders.

Loren burned with conflicting emotions. He hadn't shot a man before. He didn't know if he'd killed him or not, but the rush, the terrible thrill of it, hummed in his veins. It felt good... and for that, he felt shame.

The Rubies had taught him how to ride long nights without sleep, how to fire Colts and Winchesters until the barrel smoked, and how to read the desert sky for rain. They taught him skills to survive in the harsh territory. They gave him a place to belong. Yet somehow, this morning, riding home through the canyon with his new family, Loren felt all alone.

3

Arizona Territory – 1877

The copper veins near Globe had begun to draw men into the mountains and already the town was swollen with tents, crude wooden shacks, and the stink of mule dung. Smoke from cookfires mixed with the dust of pickaxes and blasting powder. At night, the town's single row of saloons came alive, lanterns glowing like beacons in the dark hills.

It was at the far end of Broad Street, where the lanterns gave way to shadow, that the Rubies found themselves. The saloon leaned against the hillside as if it might collapse, but inside the air was thick with pipe smoke, whiskey, and the fever of men who had worked hard and meant to lose even harder.

Loren sat near the wall, his guitar in his lap. The strings hummed low, a Spanish ballad twisted through his Cajun tongue. His notes floated through the din, earning him a few coins tossed lazily into his hat. But he was watching more than he was playing, keeping one eye on his brothers at the tables.

Mateo and Red stood at the bar, backs to the room, drinking steadily but never truly drunk. Cobb and John had taken a table near the back, cards in hand. Their winnings were growing—a neat little pile of silver dollars, folded bills, and even a small pouch of ore dust. To some men in the room, the Rubies' luck seemed to sour the air—Loren could feel the mood shift and see eyes narrowing their way.

One particular gambler had been riding the streak of bad fortune all night. A dandy out of Prescott, he wore a checkered vest and a bowler hat, his mustache neatly groomed and curled, his fingers heavy with silver rings. He'd come to Globe to skin miners of their wages, but he hadn't expected competition.

When John dragged another pot toward himself, the man slammed his fist on the table.

"Cheater!" his voice cracked above the noise. He pointed a ringed finger at John. "This varmint's been playing us for fools all night!"

The room stilled. Chairs scraped. The miners at the table straightened, their whiskey-sodden cheer turning hard.

John's eyes flared beneath the brim of his hat. He calmly set his cards down. John's eyes barely flickered beneath the brim of his hat—steady and contained. There was something about that calm that both intrigued and unsettled Loren. "Callin' me a cheat, are you?"

The cowboy sitting beside him rose halfway, a long knife flashing in the lamplight. "Is it true? You been swindlin' us?"

Loren's song died mid-note. His fingers instinctively moved from the strings of the guitar to the holster on his hip. Mateo and Red turned from the bar.

John pushed to his feet, "I don't need to cheat to best you." His hands remained empty but his eyes were burning. "You best think twice..."

The knife came up.

Cobb didn't wait. His revolver roared, the shot hammering through the close air. The knife-wielder lurched backward, eyes wide. A small dark spot the size of a quarter began to rapidly widen on his chest.

The saloon erupted. Miners dove for cover, chairs crashed to the floor, and the gambler in the bowler reached for his pistol. He was quick—but John was quicker. His Navy revolver cleared leather, the shot tearing into the man's ribs before he could even cock the hammer.

Everything broke loose at once. Another ranch hand lunged for a shotgun propped near the wall, but Loren's revolver barked twice, dropping him into the sawdust. Red, bellowing like a bull, grabbed a nearby stool from the bar and threw it toward the fracas. Cobb laughed, firing wild into the smoke and shouts.

Men bolted for the doors. Others ducked behind barrels and tables.

When the gun smoke thinned, Loren saw bodies scattered across the floor—too many. The Rubies stood breathing hard, guns smoking, Red's winnings spilled and scattered among blood and glass.

"Time to go," Mateo snapped.

They burst into the street, gun smoke rolling after them. Nitis was already waiting in the shadows, the horses saddled and ready. He had heard the chaos from afar and knew his brothers' ways too well.

"¡*Vámonos*!" Mateo barked.

The Rubies swung into their saddles. Loren vaulted up, clutching the reins tight as Solano galloped with the rest.

Up the street, a bell began to ring. A voice shouted, "Marshal! Marshal!" Lanterns flared. Men spilled from saloons, some with rifles in hand. The Rubies thundered past, shots chasing them into the dark. Splinters flew as bullets struck hitching posts and doorframes. Loren ducked low, the cold wind tearing his eyes.

They rode hard through the brush, the silhouettes of the Pinal Mountains black against the moon. Branches whipped at their faces, hooves crushed cactus, but the posse's shouts faded behind them.

They didn't slow until the lights of Globe were far behind and the cold mountain air bit through their coats. At last Mateo called for a trot, then a halt near a dry arroyo lined with mesquite.

The men dismounted, breath steaming in the chill night. Cobb grinned, his revolver still warm in his hand. "Hell of a night, eh boys?"

John rounded on him. "You son of a bitch! I had it handled. You didn't need to kill that man."

"He had a knife coming at your ribs. What was I supposed to do? Watch?"

"You were supposed to wait for me to deal with it! He was bluffing.... I saw the same twitch of his upper lip during the game."

"Enough," Mateo barked, his voice cutting sharp. "You both brought blood we didn't need. Now the marshal's got half the town riled, and the law will be hunting us."

Cobb smirked, unbothered. John paced, fists clenched.

Loren stayed silent, still hearing the gunshots ringing in his head. He could still see the look on the gambler's face when John's bullet struck him and the knife-wielder's eyes frozen in shock as his life drained out.

Mateo glanced at Loren—both quiet and distant—and laid a hand on his shoulder. "You'll see more nights like this, *hermano*. Best get used to the sound."

The fire crackled. Above, the moon climbed cold and white, and Loren wondered if the desert itself was watching, weighing every drop of blood spilled in its dust.

By dawn, the Rubies were already miles from Globe. The mountains gave way to high desert, creosote and prickly pear scattered among dry washes. The sun rose harsh and white, gilding the rocky peaks in fire.

They rode east at first, then bent south to throw off any pursuers. The trail carried them along the edge of the San Carlos Apache Reservation, where the army had forced whole bands into confinement. Smoke curled from distant camps, and the men rode in silence, each knowing better than to linger near the patrols that shadowed the place.

"Law'll hang a man for less than a card game," Red muttered, spitting into the dust.

Mateo kept his eyes forward. "All the more reason we keep moving."

It was Nitis who finally broke the long silence. The Apache had ridden half a mile ahead, his eyes scanning every ridge and wash. When he returned to the group, his voice was low and measured.

"You spill blood in a mining town, the ground remembers," he said, glancing from Mateo to Loren. "Men think they can bury their sins, but the desert does not bury. It only keeps."

Loren frowned, chewing on the words. "What's that supposed to mean?"

Nitis fixed him with a stare as sharp as obsidian. "Every man you kill walks beside you after. Some louder than others. You will hear them when you try to sleep."

Cobb laughed from the rear. "Ain't no ghosts walking beside me. Just whiskey and coin."

Nitis said nothing, but Loren thought he caught the flicker of a smile—brief and unreadable.

As they cut across a wide basin south of the Gila, Red eased his horse closer to Loren's mustang. His massive hands worked the reins loosely, and his beard was dusted pale with trail grit.

"You held your seat well last night," Red said quietly, voice like gravel.

Loren glanced at him. "Didn't feel like it. Felt like I was holdin' on to keep from pissin' myself."

Red's guffaw rolled through the still air. "That's half of what ridin' with the Rubies is. Don't let Cobb fool you—he pisses himself near every time, just too ornery to admit it."

Loren allowed himself a small grin. "You think Cobb was wrong to shoot that man?"

Red's face hardened, but he didn't look away. "Man had a knife. Cobb saved my hide, I'll give him that. But there's a difference between survival and satisfaction. Cobb don't always know the difference."

Loren nodded, the words settling into him like warm coals. Something in Red's rough kindness echoed his brother—the one he'd lost at Shiloh.

The two rode in silence for a while, the sound of hooves and the whistle of wind their only company. It was near dark when the spire of the old mission rose from the desert. Half buried in sand and shadow, its cracked adobe walls glowed faintly in the sunset. Crows wheeled overhead, their calls harsh against the stillness.

The Rubies rode into the courtyard, dust trailing behind them. The old bell still hung in the tower, though it hadn't tolled in decades. Loren dismounted stiffly, brushing the sweat from Solano's neck.

Inside the churchyard, the men set about making camp. Mateo poured mezcal into tin cups. Cobb went for the firewood, muttering curses. John sat apart, methodical as always, reloading his revolvers. Nitis slipped into the brush without a word—there one moment, gone the next—keeping watch somewhere beyond the firelight.

Loren strummed a few chords on his guitar, the notes echoing strangely against the broken stone. Red lowered himself beside him, his huge frame creaking like a barn door. Red sat heavily on a stone, wiping sweat from his brow. He looked at Loren.

Loren kept his head down . "I don't really know what happened... just reacted."

"That's how it starts," Red said, his tone both kind and grim. "You'll tell yourself you can stop when you want. But every trigger you pull makes the next one easier. Remember that." He paused. "Now play somethin' not so sad. World's heavy enough."

Loren smiled faintly and shifted into a quicker tune, one of the jigs his brother used to fiddle on the banks of the Atchafalaya. Red clapped along, beard shaking with laughter.

For the first time since the smoke and blood in Globe, Loren felt the tightness in his chest ease. Around him the Rubies laughed, drank, and argued—their voices rising under the desert stars.

The mission was crumbling, the law was now surely hunting, but in that moment, they were a family. And for the first time, Loren felt it clear as the desert stars—the boy with the guitar and the trembling hand—he was one of them.

4

New Mexico Territory – 1877

The Rubies cut across the desert with the steady patience Loren had come to expect from men who knew exactly how far a horse could go before breaking. The land around them stretched wide and harsh—mesquite and ocotillo clinging to arroyos, distant ridges baked red under the morning sun. Buzzards drifted on high currents, shadows circling on the ground below.

Loren sat high in the saddle, his eyes searching the horizon. Still a young man, he was quickly learning how to survive in the territory. Each day brought a new experience—a new opportunity to learn—and most days Loren felt like he was drinking from a well that never emptied—every mile teaching him something new. His skills as a rider and a marksman had improved considerably and the others could see the increased confidence in his eyes. But he wasn't hardened by the desert—or the outlaw life—he was adapting to it.

Mateo led from the front, his broad shoulders easy in the saddle. "This one will be different," he called over the thud of hooves. "No guns, no chases. Just cloth and coin."

"Cloth don't fill a man's belly," Cobb muttered.

"It fills his pockets," Mateo said, undeterred. "We carry fabric to El Paso, deliver it clean, and walk away richer than we came."

Red's laugh carried through the dry air. "And if it's that easy, Mateo, why didn't you fetch it yourself?"

"Because, *hermano*. I know how to plan, but a plan still needs men to ride it out."

John's eyes stayed on the horizon, his voice even as a drawn blade. "No plan survives men with guns and pride."

Loren kept close to Red, listening but saying nothing. He'd been riding with them long enough to know that "easy" was a word the desert always twisted into something else.

By midday the gang reached the Rio Grande, broad and shallow where they forded. Across the water lay Juárez, a jumble of adobe houses, tiled roofs, and dust-choked streets. Market stalls pressed against one another like cattle in a pen, the air full of the scent of roasting peppers, sweat, and horse dung.

Children ran between wagons, women shouted prices for pottery and fruit, and soldiers leaned in the shade of walls, their rifles propped against their knees. Juárez was alive in a way that made Loren's head spin—too many voices, too many eyes.

Mateo led them to a warehouse painted in fading blue, its wooden doors sagging. A portly man with a gleaming white mustache stood waiting—Don Emilio Vargas.

"¡Mateo!" Emilio boomed, embracing him. "You bring your boys. Fine riders, eh?"

The introductions were quick. Inside, bolts of cloth lay stacked floor to rafters—silks from Veracruz, cotton dyed in deep crimsons and indigos, even lace fine enough for a church veil. Loren touched one of the bolts, astonished by its softness. It felt like a dream in his hands, fragile and impossible.

"Handle it gently," Emilio chuckled. "That's worth more than you are, *chico*."

The Rubies loaded the cloth on their packhorses, securing the bundles tight. When the last knot was cinched, Emilio clapped Mateo on the back. "Get this to my partners across the border and you'll be paid well."

They crossed the Rio Grande again by a ford west of town. Halfway across, two *rurales* appeared, rifles resting casual on their shoulders.

"*¿A dónde van?*" one asked sharply.

Mateo dipped his hat. "Just gifts for El Paso ladies. Nothing more." He produced a bottle of mezcal and held it up with a grin.

The *rurales* shared a look, then laughed. One took the bottle, uncorking it for a swig. "*Vayan.*" He waved them on.

"See?" Mateo said as they rode clear. "Always cheaper to buy smiles than bullets."

Cobb spat into the dirt. "Till the smiles run dry."

By late afternoon they entered El Paso. Unlike Juárez, the town had an angular stiffness—clapboard storefronts with painted signs, wide dusty streets with horse-drawn wagons, and soldiers in Union blue pacing near the railyard. The air carried the clang of iron rails and the acrid scent of coal smoke.

Loren's eyes darted everywhere—to the gamblers leaning against the saloon doors and to the women in bright dresses stepping over ruts in the street. Compared to Nogales or Tubac, El Paso felt larger, louder, and bristling with a hunger that matched the desert wind.

The warehouse by the railyard was little more than a wooden barn with tall doors. Inside, two Anglo merchants waited. Their coats were pressed, collars starched, hair slick with oil. Their soft hands told Loren they'd never known a day of work in the sun. The merchants weren't alone, though. A half dozen workers moved about the warehouse, barely glancing at the deal taking place.

Two burly men in work shirts and suspenders stood near the back of the warehouse, rifles resting casually in their hands—and Loren noticed John's gaze linger on a beat too long. "Hired muscle," he muttered to Loren.

The merchants counted each bundle of cloth, marking ledgers with bored precision. Mateo stood nearby, arms crossed, face calm but watchful.

"The price was agreed," Mateo said when the tally ended. "You've got the goods. Pay us."

One of the merchants adjusted his spectacles. "Market's shifted. Half payment will suffice."

Cobb's face reddened. "Half?" His hand drifted to his gun. Red placed a massive hand on Cobb's shoulder, holding him back. "Easy now."

But Mateo's voice cut through. "Our agreement was set. Cheat me, and you insult more than a contract."

The merchant shrugged. "Then consider yourself insulted."

That was the spark. Cobb drew first, firing before Red could stop him. The bullet slammed into the merchant's chest, sending him sprawling. John's revolver was out in the same instant, his shot driving the second merchant behind a crate.

"Down!" Mateo barked, shoving Loren behind a crate just as the first shot cracked past. Splinters flew, stinging his cheek.

Cobb ducked and fired wild, his bullet smashing through stacked fabric. John moved quick and exact—two shots, two men going down before Loren could blink. One of the guards fell hard to the floor, the other howling as his shoulder burst red. The wounded guard kept shooting, stumbling as he fought to stay upright. His round slammed into a crate near Red, spraying cloth and dust.

Red bellowed, rage flaring, and swung his shotgun from his back. The blast thundered in the enclosed space, ripping a hole clean through the man's chest. He hit the ground with a grunt that rattled Loren's bones.

Loren crouched low, heart hammering. His pistol felt like a stone in his hand. He saw the last merchant scrambling for cover behind a barrel, his face white as chalk. For a moment, Loren's finger twitched on the trigger—but he froze.

"Shoot him, boy!" Cobb shouted, eyes wild.

But Loren couldn't.... The merchant wasn't armed, after all. He aimed at the dirt instead, the bullet kicking up dust. Before the merchant could rise, Cobb's revolver exploded once more. The man dropped, lifeless, ledger still clutched in his hand.

That was when the lantern tipped.

A spilled bolt of cotton caught fire, the flames racing fast. Within seconds the flames licked the walls, turning each bolt of fabric into bright bursts. The warehouse filled with smoke and heat, the cloth curling and blackening. The dyes in the fabrics released a sickly, choking smell as they burned, colors bleeding into the air.

"Move!" Mateo roared. He grabbed Loren by the collar and dragged him toward the doors. Cobb fired a last shot at the burning piles, laughing as if the blaze were his handiwork. Red cursed, hauling another crate aside to clear their exit. "Get out!" he shouted.

The Rubies, faces blackened with soot, spilled into the street as the townsfolk panicked. Women screamed, children darted for doorways, and men fled down the street. The flames leaped through the warehouse roof, lighting the sky orange.

Soldiers down the way turned at the sound of shouts rising. One of the officers shouted orders and rifles snapped to their shoulders. They began running hard toward the warehouse.

Nitis was across the street in an alleyway with the horses. Sitting atop his own mount, he let out a piercing whistle that carried across the chaos and noise. Mateo caught a glimpse of Nitis and quickly motioned for the others. "Juanito, Red…. This way. *¡Vamos!*"

The Rubies sprinted for their waiting mounts. Nitis, slowly and calmly, drew an arrow to his bow and released. Although he was highly proficient with a rifle, he preferred the silent strike of an arrow. Cobb shoved a bystander into the dirt. Loren fired a single shot overhead. The sound cracked like thunder, scattering the crowd in every direction. A horse bolted from its hitching post, kicking over barrels and adding to the chaos.

Bullets whined past the Rubies as they mounted their horses. One shot smashed into the sign of a saloon, another chipped stone by Loren's stirrup. He hunched low against Solano's neck, praying the mustang's speed would carry him out alive.

They fled north at a dead gallop, smoke trailing into the sky behind them. Fire still glowed against the darkening sky behind them, El Paso's streets alive with chaos. Loren clung to Solano's reins, heart hammering. Cobb laughed like a madman, spurring his horse harder, while John's eyes stayed flat and cold.

The Rubies rode hard, dust boiling up in their wake, until the lights of town were nothing but a smear on the horizon. By midnight they reached the shadow of Mammoth Rock, a jagged outcrop that loomed black against the stars. The men dismounted, horses lathered and trembling.

Mateo paced, furious. "No payment. No goods. A fire that'll have soldiers on our trail by dawn. This was supposed to be simple!"

Cobb shrugged. Firelight flickered across his grinning face, stretched too wide to look natural. "Shouldn't have cheated us."

Red wheeled on him. "You couldn't hold your hand?!"

"They cheated us," Cobb repeated tersely. "I ain't a man who lets that stand. I gave 'em what they earned."

John's voice cut like a knife. "You gave us nothing but enemies."

Red moved over to where Loren was sitting, plopped down on the cold dirt, and pulled his hat down low. Loren had been strumming a few chords on his guitar.

Cobb walked over and kicked Loren's leg. "Why'd you pause on that sum'bitch? He had it coming."

Loren didn't look up—just continued plucking at the strings. "He wasn't armed."

"Makes no difference," Cobb replied coldly. He turned and walked away.

Red lifted the brim of his hat. "You keep your head, kid. You got the makings of somethin' better than just another killer." The words surprised Loren, more than he wanted to show.

Nitis, who had ridden silent the whole way, finally spoke. "The desert keeps its debts. Tonight, we owe more than coin."

Loren didn't reply, and neither did anyone else. For a long moment, the only sound was the fire popping. Cobb muttered something about finding whiskey and stomped away from the fire.

Loren tilted his head back, staring at the stars overhead. His hands still shook from the heat of the warehouse, the memory of silk turning to ash. Easy money, Mateo had promised. But all Loren could see was smoke... and wanted posters with his face—and the face of his family—on them. He thought of Nitis's warning—about ghosts that never left a man alone—and he wondered how many were already walking beside him.

5

New Mexico Territory – 1877

Las Cruces shimmered under the punishing sun—the Organ Mountains jagged against the sky like teeth. The Rubies had been laying low in a mesquite thicket outside town, their horses restless—and from the way the men snapped at small things and stared too long at the horizon, Loren guessed their tempers were restless too. After El Paso, Loren found himself hoping for something cleaner—a job that didn't end in smoke and ash.

Mateo sat cross-legged in the dust, a stick scratching crude lines in the dirt. The others leaned in, studying his drawing.

"The train rolls east from Deming every Friday," he explained. "Freight and passengers. Rich passengers." He tapped a thick line with the stick. "Here, outside Las Cruces, the track climbs slow. We block it with timber. Train stops. Cobb takes the engine, Nitis watches the land, and we walk off with whatever shines."

Red scratched his beard. "Quick in, quick out."

"Quick in, quick out," Mateo echoed. "Smooth as silk."

Cobb grinned. "And no damned merchants to argue price."

John's sharp eyes flicked to Loren. "Think you're ready to play a different tune, *muchacho*?" Loren's hand brushed the guitar at his side. He wasn't sure if John meant music or bullets. "I'll keep the rhythm," he said softly.

The desert air was unusually cool. Clouds slowly passed by overhead, blocking the sun as it traveled toward the western horizon. They stayed by the tracks, watching... waiting. When the whistle finally echoed from the west, Mateo raised his hand.

"Now."

Red and Cobb hauled a felled log onto the rails. The locomotive screeched and shuddered to a halt, hissing steam like some wounded beast.

Cobb scrambled up into the engine, swinging his pistol. "Hands up!" he barked, cracking the conductor across the skull with his revolver butt. The man crumpled. The fireman froze.

Mateo and Red moved fast to the rear passenger car, their boots pounding on the gravel. John nudged Loren toward the next car. "Your stage awaits, troubadour."

Inside, gas lamps lit the faces of startled passengers. A woman gasped, clutching pearls. A man rose, fists clenched.

Loren strummed his guitar, voice steady though his heart hammered. "No one needs to bleed tonight. Sit quiet, stay calm, and you'll live to tell the tale." His Cajun drawl stretched into Spanish verse—half song, half command.

John moved aisle to aisle, his pistols gleaming, plucking watches and purses with practiced grace. For a moment, it seemed to work. The passengers froze—eyes fixed on Loren's guitar or on the guns.

Then two young men rose from their seats, one grabbing John's arm, the other swinging a fist. One of John's revolvers clattered to the floor.

John cursed, struggling to fight off both men. Other passengers started to move and rise from their seats. Loren stopped strumming. Sensing the situation and the building tension, his hand went to his holster, his body moving before his mind caught up. Two shots cracked. The two young men collapsed, blood soaking the carpet.

The car fell into silence, the air thick with smoke. The passengers were frozen, no one moved. Loren looked down at the bodies. Maybe they meant to be heroes, but the desert—and Loren—didn't grant them the part.

Then Loren heard it—the scuff of boots behind him. "Behind you!" John shouted. He spun just as another man lunged with a knife. Loren fired. The man dropped at his feet, blade skittering across the floorboards.

John retrieved his pistol, giving Loren a sharp nod. "Well done, *muchacho*."

The praise buzzed through Loren like lightning. His ears rang, his chest heaved, but his hands were steady now.

They gathered what they could, shoving jewelry and purses into saddlebags, and leaped from the train as Mateo and Red came running from their car, already heavy with loot.

Nitis whistled sharp from a small ridge nearby, signaling clear ground. Horses stamped, ready to run.

"Ride!" Mateo bellowed.

The Rubies vanished toward the setting sun, the train shrinking behind them.

They rode north hard, laughter and curses filling the night air. Cobb whooped like a madman. "Now that's outlaw work!" he shouted, eyes gleaming. "Our little singer's growin' teeth!"

John reined in beside Loren, his tone quieter but more piercing. "Clean shots, fast reflexes. You didn't hesitate. That'll keep you alive."

Red clapped Loren on the back so hard he nearly lost his seat. "Brother, you looked like a man born for the saddle and the smoke. Drinks on me when we hit Silver City!"

Loren said nothing. His heart raced, but it wasn't fear anymore. It was exhilaration, a rush so fierce he thought his veins might burst. For the first time, he felt like he wasn't just riding with the Rubies—he *was* one of them.

By the time dawn touched the land, they had reached the looming mass of Cookes Peak. They made camp in a canyon, firelight flickering on the granite walls. The horses grazed on sparse grass, their sides heaving from the long push.

Mateo poured mezcal, passing tin cups around. "A clean score," he said. "No wagons, no merchants, no fire. This is how it should be."

John's gaze lingered on Loren. "You did well today. There's no going back from it."

Loren stared into the fire. "I didn't think. I just... did it."

"You relied on your skills." John took out the revolver that fell to the floor of the passenger car and examined it.

"That's how it begins," Red said gently. "I told ya, it gets easier each time. Too easy, sometimes. That's the danger."

Silence fell heavy around the fire until Nitis finally spoke. His voice was low and patient, carrying across the canyon like wind. "The boy has killed. Now the desert will weigh him."

Loren looked up. "Weigh me?"

"The land keeps account. It marks those who take life, even when the taking feels right. You must learn to carry the weight of the dead, or it will break you."

The next morning, as they broke camp, Nitis stiffened, eyes narrowing toward the ridges. A faint line of smoke rose along the horizon—far off, moving slow across the land. Moments later, the shapes of riders appeared—a small band of Apaches. There were half a dozen men, lean and ragged, driving stolen cattle north.

Nitis mounted without a word and rode out to meet them. The rest of the Rubies hung back, hands close to their guns... tense and curious.

The riders slowed as Nitis approached, their ponies gaunt, their eyes sunken—their faces hard and unyielding. One of them, older, with a hawk's nose and braids streaked gray, spoke with Nitis in quick, clipped tones.

The Rubies couldn't catch a word, but the rhythm was unmistakable—a conversation of equals. At last, the two clasped forearms. When Nitis returned, his expression was grave. "They are San Carlos people. They escaped many nights ago. The soldiers hunt them. They ride to find freedom or death."

Red frowned.

Nitis continued, "They will not last a week without food and cover. A little ammunition."

Mateo reached into his saddlebag and pulled out a biscuit. "Everyone, grab a little out of your bags. We can spare some now... and buy more later with the money we got from the train." Going from person to person, he collected food donations for the weary strangers.

Cobb put his hand up to stop Mateo when he approached. "They should just go back to the reservation if they want to live," Cobb said flatly. "What's in my bag is mine."

Mateo squinted his eyes and shook his head in disapproval. "They are what we claim to be—men refusing chains. If we are true to ourselves, we help." When Cobb didn't reach into his saddlebag, Mateo shrugged his shoulders, then turned and handed the collection to Nitis to give to the Apache riders.

"Being alive is not the same as living. Being free is living... and freedom is worth bleeding for," Nitis replied. "These men know it. Do you?" His eyes fixed on Loren.

The boy swallowed hard. "I think so."

"Then learn," Nitis said. "A man is only free when he knows who he is. Without that, he's just another captive, even with a gun in his hand. You are not yet stone," he added. "The desert has not hardened you. You can still decide what freedom means."

He turned, gesturing toward the ragged riders waiting under the ridge. "To them, freedom is the chance to ride and die on their own land. To you—what is it? Gold? Songs? Solitude? Is it loyalty to men who will one day lie in the dust?"

The words stuck a chord within Loren. His hand tightened on Solano's reins. He thought of his mother's voice back on the Atchafalaya, of Red's rough laughter beside the fire, of the thrill when his pistol struck true on the train. He had no answer.

Red clapped Loren on the shoulder. "Don't twist yourself up, brother. Freedom's what you make it."

Nitis carried the supplies back to the Apaches. The old man accepted the gift with a nod, no words wasted. Then the band moved on, vanishing into the scrub like shadows.

When Nitis returned, Cobb shook his head. "You'll never see that food or powder again."

Nitis gazed off toward the horizon, his face unreadable. "It was never ours to keep."

Loren carried the exchange long into the ride northwest—the words churned in his head, like a song he couldn't forget. The thrill of the train robbery still lingered inside him, but now it was tempered by something else—the weight Nitis spoke of, what it meant to be free. *Am I free*, he thought, *or am I chained to the excitement?*

They pushed northwest, the mountains rising before them, the air growing colder. Silver City glittered somewhere ahead, a town fat with miners' wages and merchants' greed.

Mateo rode at the head, grinning. "This is only the beginning, *hermanos*. The desert sings when we ride it. And today it sings of victory!"

Mateo wasn't wrong, but he wasn't exactly correct either. Loren had started to hear whispers in towns across the territory—talk of a gang that rode like ghosts and left trouble in their wake. The small inconsequential jobs that had been their custom were nothing more than nuisance to locals, but the more recent events had resulted in property damage and death. The law had begun to take notice.

Loren glanced at the others—Cobb's reckless grin, John's sharp calm, Red's broad laughter, Nitis's silent gaze—and wondered which of them he was destined to become.

For now, he let Solano carry him forward, his heart pounding with the rhythm of the hooves.

6

New Mexico Territory – 1877

Silver City sat in the basin like a beacon, its buildings stacked of brick and timber rather than sunbaked adobe. Lanterns glowed along the boardwalks, and miners swaggered through the streets, boots loud on planks, pockets fat with wages earned in the shafts that clawed at the Gila Mountains.

Ore wagons creaked past at all hours, mules straining against the harness. Dust hung in the air like smoke. Posters flapped on the walls—railroad schedules, boxing bouts, sermons, reward notices. At night the town hummed like a hive, the saloons bursting with rough laughter and piano music that fought to be heard above it. Men came here to get rich, lose it fast, and pretend it never mattered.

Loren lived like a man reborn into a life of comfort. The Rubies lodged at the Palace Hotel, its brass chandeliers glittering with oil lamps, carpets soft enough to make Loren think of river moss under bare feet. Behaving like a gentleman, Loren paid his daily hotel bill using crisp greenbacks acquired from the train robbery.

He learned the quiet rituals of town life again—linen napkins folded like doves, waiters who called him *sir*, polished boots lined at the door. Sometimes he caught his reflection in a gilt mirror and hardly knew the man staring back. Outlaw. Gentleman. Saint. Sinner. It was all a matter of which room he was standing in.

On the first night in town, Mateo clapped Loren on the back. "Come, *hermano*. Time you learned how the other half smells."

They went together to the bathhouse. Steam filled the air, mingling with the sharp bite of lye soap. Loren sank into the hot water, hissing as the heat bit into trail-worn skin. It was the first true bath he'd had since leaving Louisiana.

In the bathhouse, steam rose in thick clouds. Mateo leaned back, water lapping at his scarred chest, and let out a groan that echoed like thunder.

"This, *hermano*," he said, "is why we ride, why we bleed. Not for dust and beans, but for glory. A man who lives like this, even just a week, lives better than a priest in his whole life." He groaned in delight, leaning back. "A man must have glory, and glory means living like a king when you can."

Loren stared at the rising steam. "Glory don't last. The water turns cold, and you end up in the dust again."

Mateo chuckled, slapping the surface so it splashed. "Ah, but kings for a day are still kings. That's what matters."

Loren looked at his reflection in the rippling surface and smiled faintly. The words sank into him. They unsettled him—and tempted him, too, though he hated to admit it. Somewhere deep inside, he wondered which of them was right—the man chasing glory, or the man afraid of it.

For weeks, they kept quiet. The Rubies played at being ordinary men, drifting through saloons, eating steak dinners, sleeping in clean beds. Cobb drank too much and courted fights in saloons, though Mateo reined him in before iron cleared leather. Nitis disappeared into the hills by day, returning only after dark with dust in his hair. Red spent his nights at the billiards hall, laughing until his beard shook. John wrote careful notes in a small ledger. But Loren knew the leisure was only a mask. Mateo was planning.

Every day, the Rubies watched the Silver City Bank from different vantage points. Freight wagons rattled past, clerks hurried with ledgers, and ladies in feathered hats stepped neatly around horse dung as if sin itself might be catching. Mateo and John strolled by on opposite sides of Main Street, hats low, eyes sharp. Red lingered at the café across the way, a steaming cup untouched as he studied the guards. Loren sat in the hotel parlor with his guitar, plucking soft tunes while glancing through the curtains at the building across the street. They learned when guards changed shifts, how the tellers left at dusk, and which alleyways lay shadowed.

Patterns emerged—two armed guards inside, one patrolling the boardwalk, all relieved at noon and dusk. The tellers left at six sharp, carrying their ledgers in leather satchels. The marshal walked the south end of Main Street most evenings, pausing at the same saloon for a whiskey before dusk. Deputies drifted in pairs, but only after the lamps were lit.

One afternoon, John strode through the bank doors in his dark suit and black hat, his pistols hidden beneath the coat. He looked like any other customer—at least to anyone who didn't know better. He laid bills from the train robbery onto the counter. "I'd like to open an account," he said, his voice even.

The teller smiled politely, sliding a ledger toward him. John signed with a flourish, though his sharp eyes were not on the paper. They flicked to the vault in the corner, iron-bellied, a guard posted nearby. He noted the brass lamp above, the narrow alcove, the thick walls. When he stepped back into the sunlight, he already had the vault etched in memory.

That evening, over drinks in their hotel room, John sketched it in charcoal. Mateo traced the lines with his thick finger, eyes glinting. "This is not brute work. This one requires precision. Timing, silence, control."

After days of careful observation and planning, the time had come. Mateo had chosen to execute the heist on the new moon—when the night sky would be dark-est. Their plan seemed quiet and simple enough—kidnap a bank employee and coerce the teller to unlock the doors and safe.

Preparations for the escape had been set up during the day, and by evening the Rubies were lying in wait on a shadowed street. The lamps hissed faintly, a dog barked somewhere down an alley.

The chosen teller was a thin man with a waxed mustache who walked home alone. He walked briskly from the bank, satchel in hand. He glanced nervously at every shadow, though he had no reason yet to suspect danger.

Red stepped out first, his bulk blotting the lamplight. "Evenin', friend."

The teller stiffened. Before he could cry out, Loren pressed a pistol to his back. "Quiet," he murmured. His voice was calm, almost a lullaby. "Walk with us."

John gripped his collar as they ushered him quietly to the rear of the bank, the man stammering prayers. Mateo slipped the keyring from his trembling fingers.

"Please," the man whispered, his breath quick. "I've a family."

Mateo's tone was almost fatherly. "Do as you're told and you'll see them again. Now, open the door."

The frightened teller took the keys from Mateo's hand. Fumbling for a moment, he nearly dropped the key ring. Mateo was growing impatient. The teller composed himself and inserted the key into the lock. The tumblers clicked. The door creaked open into darkness.

Inside, the bank was still, the air smelled of ink and iron. Somewhere in the darkness, the brass clock on the wall ticked like a heartbeat. Their boots echoed on the polished floorboards, and their shadows stretched long as they made their way toward the large vault in the corner. The teller begged for his life as they forced him onward.

When they reached the vault, John pushed him forward. "Open it."

The man shook his head. "Only the manager knows the combination. I swear it."

Cobb snarled, jamming his pistol under the man's chin. "He's lying."

"Leave him," Mateo ordered. "I was prepared for this possibility." His eyes shifted to Red. "Blow it."

Red knelt, hands steady as he unpacked black powder and a short fuse from a saddlebag he had draped over his shoulder. He packed the powder into the lock, lit the fuse, and stepped away. "Clear back." Loren swallowed as he and John dragged the teller aside, the man sobbing quietly into his sleeve.

The explosion rattled the bank. Dust rained from the rafters. When the smoke cleared, the heavy iron door sagged open, warped but broken. Inside lay sacks of coins, bundles of notes, even silver ingots stacked like bricks. Even in the dim light, Loren saw the gleam in everyone's eyes.

They moved quickly, stuffing saddlebags until they bulged.

The explosion was a thunderclap in the quiet night, and it had awakened the town. Shouts rose outside. Boots pounded on the boardwalk. The sharp command of deputies echoed through the night. Through the shutters on the windows, Loren saw the glow of lanterns swinging, the silhouettes of deputies taking positions across the street.

"We've got company," he muttered.

"The front door," Mateo barked. "The horses are there. We ride or we hang."

"They've got us pinned," John hissed, peering through a crack in the shutters. Lawmen crouched behind wagons and barrels across the street, rifles pointed at the bank—ready for action.

They burst through the doors into the night. John, Cobb, and Loren laid down cover, pistols flashing. John and Loren shot in unison, driving the deputies back. Cobb fired wild, teeth clenched. The deputies fired back, bullets sparking off the hitching posts. One slug caught Cobb in the shoulder, spinning him into the dirt. He snarled as he staggered to his feet. Red pulled him upright with one massive arm.

Nitis's arrows—coming from a location down the street—whistled through the smoke, felling two men before they could fire again.

Loren felt the air crackle around him as lead split the night. He aimed and fired, driving a deputy back into the alley. Another shot came close, grazing his ear.

Behind him, Mateo and Red shoved the heavy bags of money onto the horses. The animals reared, eyes wild from the smoke.

"Mount!" Mateo roared.

The Rubies vaulted into their saddles. They spurred hard, horses thundering down the main street as gunfire echoed behind them. Loren clutched Solano's reins, heart hammering. Dust and noise swallowed the world. As they escaped south, a bullet tore into Loren's back—not flesh, but wood. His guitar, slung across his

shoulders, exploded in splinters. Loren gasped, clutching the ruined neck as if it were a wound. It felt, for one
sharp second, like the last good part of him had been
shot away. The strings twanged their last note, and the
bank, the lawmen, the shouting—all of it—vanished
behind him into the night.

7

New Mexico Territory – 1877

For two days, they rode through scrubland and arroyos, resting only long enough to water the horses before pressing on. The sacks of money weighed heavy, not just on the animals but on every mind in the gang. The desert seemed alive with echoes—every dust plume on the horizon felt like riders closing in. Even the wind sounded like hoofbeats when it swept the gravel plains.

They made camp at Burro Peak, firelight dancing on their grins as they counted their spoils. The mountain rose like a black tooth against the stars, cutting the night sky into hard edges. Spirits soared, the air filled with Red's booming laugh, Cobb's bitter curses at his wound, and Mateo's boasting. Loren, however, was more melancholic. His guitar was in pieces. His song, his shield—gone. He felt the loss like a knife to his chest.

When the Rubies broke camp the next day, all the talk centered around how each would spend his share. Little thought was given to how they had gotten their riches. But Silver City was not quick to forget. Its wrath was relentless. Near the town of Lordsburg, the Rubies were reminded of the fury they thought they'd left behind.

From a rise, Loren saw it first—a line of men kicking up dust and sunlight flashing on rifle barrels. A posse caught their trail. Armed townsfolk and deputies were pushing hard toward the gang, rifles cracking. These weren't men chasing after a legend destined for a wanted poster. These were men chasing stolen wages, justice, and pride.

"Riders behind us!" he shouted.

Mateo cursed and spurred his horse. "Push on, *hermanos*!"

The Rubies kicked their mounts into a gallop, hooves pounding over hardpan. The posse fanned out, shouting, their voices faint over the wind. Bullets cracked, spitting dirt near Solano's hooves.

The chase ripped through the desert, bullets whining like angry hornets. Loren clung low to his mustang's neck. A bullet struck Loren's leg, grazing the flesh, fire searing through him. He clenched his teeth and clung to Solano, refusing to fall. His leg burned, the sting of blood hot against his trousers. Each jolt of the saddle sent a knife of pain through him, but he refused to falter.

John twisted in his saddle, cool as ever. He fired two shots, driving a pursuer back. Cobb, pale from his shoulder wound, let out a ragged laugh. "Come on, you bastards!" he hollered, emptying a revolver at shadows too far to hit.

The chase carried them into a narrow wash where the mesquite grew thick. Nitis raised his hand, signaling a split in the land ahead. "There!"

They veered toward a ravine, its walls jagged and close. Horses scrambled down, stone breaking under their hooves. The posse tried to follow, but the trail narrowed, and two of their mounts balked, rearing at the drop.

Dust boiled up, cloaking the Rubies. Mateo whooped, the sound echoing off stone. They drove their horses hard, weaving through the canyon until the gunfire behind faded into silence. By the time they climbed back onto open land, the sun was sinking, casting long shadows across the desert. They had shaken the posse—for now—but Loren didn't relax. Chases didn't end. They only fell behind.

The ride east was long and hard, but the mountains welcomed them like dark sentinels. By the time they reached the Chiricahuas, the air grew cooler and the scent of pine mingled with desert sage. The Rubies allowed themselves to rest—to breathe again, laughter rising under the shadow of the peaks. They made camp among the granite spires of the range, the night air sharp with the scent of piñon and juniper. A fire crackled low, the glow soft against their weary faces.

Cobb nursed his shoulder with a bottle of whiskey, swearing between gulps. "Silver City won't forget us," he muttered. "Marshal'll have wanted posters hung in every town across the territory."

Red chuckled, beard twitching with his grin. "Then we'll be famous, eh? Men will sing our names in cantinas."

"Or curse them," John said, reloading each pistol with his usual calm.

Nitis sat apart, sharpening a knife, his voice quiet when it came. "The desert tests us... always."

Loren stared into the fire, the shattered remains of his guitar sitting by his side. The pain in his leg throbbed with each heartbeat, but it was nothing compared to the hollow ache in his chest. He reached for a stick, poking at the fire until sparks leaped into the cool night air.

The next day, they descended from the Chiricahuas, the land opening again into wide desert. It took another week, but they rode back into their ruined mission hideout with sacks of coin and tales to tell.

They spilled the loot across a battered table, coins glinting in the lamplight. Cobb drank to his survival, Mateo roared about destiny, Red clapped John's back until he coughed. The celebration was fierce, mezcal flowing, laughter spilling into the night.

Loren sat apart from the gang, staring at the shattered fragments of his guitar. He had been unable to discard the remains during the long ride back to the hideout. Looking now at what was left of it, he realized there was a cost to living the outlaw life. Sitting there in the crumbling walls of the mission, he saw the truth—the desert had stripped away the last of who he thought he was. Maybe this was the path meant for him—gunpowder and blood, not songs. He rose from his seat and approached the small fire in the middle of the room. While the others were laughing and jeering, Loren quietly tossed what was left of the guitar into the flame.

***

The days passed slowly for the next few months. Winter had settled in—there was a chill in the air. The desert didn't sleep in the winter. It only held its breath. The Rubies had barely finished dividing their spoils from Silver City when Mateo began planning again. "This is just the beginning, *amigos*," he said. "But first, we rest. What good is money if we don't spend some of it, eh?"

Everyone nodded. It was decided that the gang would split up for a few months. Loren understood the reasoning. The law would be looking for a gang—not one or two random men—spending large sums of money.

Cobb had ridden off on his own shortly after the spoils were divvied up. He didn't say where he was going but Mateo suspected it was west toward a sandy beach.

Red told the group he was staying in Tucson for winter. His muscles ached and he wanted to sleep someplace comfortable. He took his share from the bank job and rode north, promising to return in the spring.

Nitis rode off toward the San Carlos reservation. He didn't say much when he left—just that he'd return. When he rode into the mission courtyard a week later, his saddlebags looked considerably lighter than when he left.

John kept a low profile and remained at the mission—occasionally venturing into Tubac when he needed supplies or Tombstone when he wanted to play cards. At the hideout, he spent his days either cleaning his revolvers or practicing with them. He wasn't a skilled woodworking craftsman like his father had been. John's craft was gunfighting and he aimed to stay sharp during the rest.

Mateo had intended on staying at the mission, but soon grew restless from the seclusion and needed the comfort of a crowd. He rode south to Nogales and camped out at the two saloons there. It did not take long for Mateo to become everyone's best friend. Whenever he had a few too many drinks—which was nearly every time—he bought a round or two for everyone in the bar.

Loren had neither a guitar to play nor a reason to use his gun. He was bored and becoming more agitated with each passing day. There were occasional rides to Nogales whenever he felt the urge to gamble, drink, or seek companionship on a lonely night—but it never fully gratified him. He felt like a knife left on a table—meant for something sharp but going dull just sitting there. The enticement of outlaw life was pulling on him. He needed a rush.

The afternoon sky was gray and cold as Loren rode north. When the white towers of San Xavier del Bac came into view—the White Dove of the Desert—he slowed Solano to a near stop. He'd ridden past the mission many times before with the gang, but this time he didn't just pass it. This time he looked at it. Really looked. The cracked white walls. The bell tower against the dull sky. He studied it.

Children played barefoot in the dust near the courtyard—their laughter thin against the sound of hunger. Loren watched them for a long moment, and something twisted in his chest.

He brought Solano to a halt and dismounted. Loren went inside the main church building. A round Jesuit priest was near the altar—his back facing the door where Loren entered. He turned when he heard the spurs singing across the floor.

The priest outstretched his arms in greeting. "Welcome, my son."

Loren pressed a heavy pouch of coins into the priest's hands. "For them," he said simply.

The priest studied him. "You walk in shadow, son. But even in shadow, the Lord leaves a light." He disappeared into the sacristy and returned with a worn guitar in his hand, its wood scarred but sturdy.

"Every soul needs a song," the priest said. "Even yours."

Loren took the instrument, strumming once. The note was raw, imperfect, but alive. He carried it out into the sunlight breaking through the clouds. He didn't know if it was salvation, but he wasn't willing to let it go.

8

Arizona Territory – 1878

Spring came to the Sonoran like a miracle. To Loren it felt strange—wrong, almost—that a land so cruel could dress itself in color. Creosote bushes dotted the plains in green, their yellow blossoms bright against the sand. Wild poppies fanned out across low valleys in rivers of orange. The air carried the sweetness of mesquite bloom, mingling with the scent of damp earth after a rare rain. Quail darted between prickly pear, their feathers flashing like little sparks of life. Even the saguaros seemed more alive, arms reaching toward a sky so blue it hurt the eyes. He knew better than to trust it.

Loren rode among it, strumming a few lazy chords on his new guitar as Solano picked his way along a rocky trail. He marveled at the blooms but couldn't escape the truth pressing on his chest—beauty did not soften the life he had chosen. No matter how bright the desert bloomed, the Rubies still rode through it like predators.

With the change of the season, the Rubies gathered once more at the old mission. Nitis spent the winter trying to teach Loren the patience of simple things—quiet mornings, clean work, long silences—but youth is stubborn, and most of those lessons slid off Loren like water from stone. John spent most of the winter at the mission too. His brief outings to the card tables had been rewarding. He frequently returned with winnings, which he carefully hid in the church. Mateo was the first among those who had fully decamped to reappear. He was heavy with ambition and light in coin, having spent too much of his Silver City take in smoky cantinas. Cobb drifted in next, riding in from Mexico—broke and bitter as ever, smelling of sweat, mezcal, and women. And then there was Red. When he returned from Tucson he didn't ride alone.

She appeared... riding beside him, her hair catching the last light of day like fire spun into gold. Rebecca Chase. Blue eyes, golden hair, a laugh sharp enough to cut a man and soft enough to heal him after. A pickpocket with hands so deft even John would come to give her a nod of respect. In Tucson, she slipped three watches and a deputy's badge from belts and pockets in the space of a single dance. Red had witnessed all of it and laughed heartily watching her, swearing she was a better thief than half the men in the territory. When he approached Rebecca later that evening it was not to turn her over to the law, but to bring her into the family.

Rebecca wasn't a whore, though the cantinas offered her coin. She wasn't a saint either. To Loren, she was a desert rose—pain dressed up as beauty. Everything he wasn't ready for.

Her first night at the abandoned mission, she teased him as he tuned his guitar. "Play something worth listening to, pretty boy. Or are you just decoration for this pack of wolves?"

Loren flushed but strummed anyway, coaxing a soft ballad into the night air. The others leaned against the ruined walls, half listening, half drunk. When the last chord faded, Rebecca stepped closer, lips near his ear.

"Careful, singer. That heart of yours might not survive this desert."

Within months, Loren had fallen into her orbit. Whether she ever truly belonged to him... he never quite believed it. Rebecca was as much the Rubies' woman as she was his, her loyalty running first to herself, second to the gang, and only then—in moments—to him. Still, he tried to hold her anyway.

By day, the Rubies moved through the mission with dull regularity. Red patched a saddle beneath the shade of the bell tower, humming an off-key hymn. John boiled coffee thick as mud in a blackened tin pot. Nitis vanished into the hills at dawn and returned at dusk with rabbits or silence, depending on what the land offered.

At night, the courtyard filled with flickering lamplight and the soft scrape of cards. Voices rose and fell. Laughter. Arguments. The ordinary music of outlaw life. Rebecca's arrival didn't shatter the routine—it slipped into it like a stone into a river, the current bending around her.

It didn't take long for her usefulness to the gang to become clear.

In addition to her pickpocket skills, she was also a distraction. Mateo quickly realized how useful that could be. When deals soured or eyes turned sharp, Rebecca's smile or her hand laid lightly on a sleeve bought the Rubies the seconds they needed. Twice, her beauty had steered suspicion away from the gang entirely.

"She's more valuable than any rifle," Mateo said one night, watching her work a crowded cantina just south of the border. "Men don't see their purses walkin' away when her eyes are on them."

Loren had bristled at the words, though he kept his face calm. He knew Mateo wasn't wrong. He also knew Rebecca would go where she pleased, and no man could hold her.

One night he found her sitting alone on the fallen church steps, staring at the cracked bell as if it might speak. The desert wind tugged at her hair. He joined her on the steps. "You ever believe in saints?" he asked.

"Once," she said. "Then I learned men build idols so they have something to blame when things go wrong... and something to kneel to when they don't want to stand on their own." She leaned her head against his shoulder without asking permission—and just as easily pulled away again. They continued talking for some time. She whispered things he had never dared to dream—a home of his own, a wife and children... a life where his guitar was all he carried.

Loren—outlaw, thief, killer, and troubadour—wanted to believe it was possible. When she got up and walked away, he stayed for a moment, watching her silhouette flicker in the moonlight.

The campfire was burning low by the time Loren approached. Red clapped him on the back. "Careful with that one," he chuckled, nodding toward Rebecca as she filched a silver ring off Cobb's finger mid-sentence. "She'll steal your wallet, your gun... and your good sense."

"Too late," Loren said, though he wasn't sure if he meant it as a joke.

Rebecca fit into the Rubies like a spark fits into dry grass. She caught quickly, burned bright, and left men wondering whether the fire would warm or consume them.

Mateo treated her as an asset. Loren could see it in the way he watched her work a crowded cantina—the same sharp attention he gave to rifles and ledgers. Rebecca wasn't just pretty to him. She was useful, and that mattered more than anything. In his ledger, she was a tool—no different than John's pistols, Nitis's arrows, or Cobb's fists. He encouraged her trickery, laughed when she charmed drunks out of silver, and studied her work with the quiet intensity of a man planning to set her at the center of bigger designs.

Red adored her—that much was obvious. He teased her relentlessly, called her "Goldilocks," and bragged like he'd discovered a gold vein himself. Sometimes Loren thought Red looked at her like a younger sister. Other times... he couldn't quite tell.

John watched her hands more than her smile. He didn't say much to her, but every now and then Loren caught a glint of approval when she slipped a purse clean. Whatever John felt, he measured it in precision—not charm.

Nitis regarded her with the same calm he gave the rest of the world. When she once pressed him, "What do you think of me, Apache?" he only said, "The desert blooms brightly before it dies." She'd laughed, but Loren had seen the shadow behind it.

Cobb, on the other hand, was loud about her—too loud. He flirted, insulted, boasted, and then tried again when she cut him down. He tried to belittle her, and she turned his insults into jokes on him that had the whole gang roaring. The more she brushed him aside, the meaner his pride seemed to grow.

Loren... he was caught somewhere between all of them. He wanted to protect her, though she needed no protection. He wanted to keep her, though she refused to be kept. And when she whispered ideas of peace, of hearth and home, he wanted to believe her—even as Mateo's voice called him back to ambition and Red's laughter kept him riding forward into danger.

***

Mateo gathered the Rubies around a low fire in the cracked courtyard of the mission—his broad shoulders hunched over a map spread across his knees. "The train was practice. The bank was a test. Now we move for something greater." His finger stabbed the map, tracing the roads that ran between Tucson and the border. "A merchant caravan. Three wagons heavy with silver ore from the Washington Camp mines. Guards, yes. Maybe soldiers, maybe hired guns. But with Becky"—he glanced at her, smiling—"with her, we have an advantage."

Rebecca leaned back, eyes glinting in the firelight. "And what part do I play in this grand show?"

"You play the lady in distress," Mateo said. "The wagons stop for you, and the rest is easy. Men with guns always think with their, um... pride... when a woman smiles."

Red snorted. "Easy, he says. Till the shooting starts."

"Then we shoot," Cobb growled, his grin not hidden at all. "Ain't nothin' new in that."

John's voice cut through, quiet but sharp. "Caravans mean escorts. Escorts mean discipline. This isn't cards or cantina pickpockets."

Mateo nodded. "We pulled one over in Silver City. We can do it again. It has to be clean. Precise. Becky draws their eyes, Loren keeps 'em calm with song, and we move before they even think to draw."

Rebecca smirked, rising to her feet. She twirled a coin between her fingers—one she'd lifted from Cobb's pocket without him noticing. "Seems I'm already earning my keep."

Cobb slapped at his vest, scowling as the others roared with laughter.

The fire had burned down to red coals when Red leaned back on his elbows, grin wide as a canyon. "You boys ever hear about the time Mateo and I tried to run a freight line?"

Mateo sighed. *"Dios mío..."*

Red barreled on anyway. "This was down near Tubac. We'd fallen in with this trader who swore there was good money haulin' barrels of lamp oil out to the mining camps. Easy pay, no risk. Only problem was, he only had one mule left—meanest animal God ever breathed life into. Looked like it was stitched together from spare parts."

John didn't look up from his cards. "So, you're the mule in this story." Laughter erupted around the fire.

Red smiled and pointed at him. "Hush." He continued, "So, there we are... me driving the cart, Mateo riding alongside tryin' to look serious like he always does. It's hotter than the devil's stovetop. We're rollin' fine until this swarm of bees comes boiling out of a mesquite tree. Turns out, bees don't rightly appreciate mule carts full of oil invading their personal space."

Loren chuckled. "What'd you do?"

"I did what any reasonable man would do," Red said proudly. "I screamed. Loud. Mule didn't like that much, so it bolts. Mateo yells something noble in Spanish and tries to grab the reins."

Mateo interrupted, "What I said was not at all noble. Sister Camila would've washed my mouth with holy water if she'd heard."

"Well, whatever said, it isn't working and he's tryin' to hang on, which is ridiculous advice when you're racin' downhill on a demon mule sittin' on top of barrels that turn the desert into one big candle," Red said. "So now the cart's bouncing like the Last Judgment and the bees are chasing us, and I'm thinkin'—this is it. This is how legends die. Smoked alive with a screaming philosopher."

Rebecca snorted behind her hand.

"We hit a rut. Cart jumps. One barrel pops loose, rolls downhill, and—swear on my sainted aunt—smashes straight into the only outhouse for twenty miles. Miner inside comes busting out with his pants around his ankles, screamin' worse than me."

"Because you nearly burned the place down," Mateo said dryly.

Red grinned brighter. "Nearly, yes. But he thanked us later. Claimed fear cured his indigestion."

John dealt a card. "And the mule?"

"Oh. That mule dragged us five more miles before stoppin' dead and takin' a nap in the middle of the road. Wouldn't move. Miners came by and paid us two dollars to leave, so technically"—he spread his hands—"it was a profitable venture."

Mateo shook his head, but there was a smile tucked in the corner of it.

"Lesson is," Red finished, raising his cup, "never trust bees, barrels, or businessmen."

Loren smiled with them, but his chest felt tight. The desert was alive with spring blossoms, yet here they were, planning to spill blood and snatch coin. Rebecca's presence only tangled him further—she made the promise of another life burn hotter, even as she bound herself to the outlaw's road.

As the firelight glimmered over the cracked mission walls, Loren wondered if he was chasing Mateo's ambition, Rebecca's smile—or something darker inside himself that wanted both the song and the smoke of gunfire.

9

Arizona Territory – 1878

The marching sun had not yet burned the mist from the arroyo when the caravan came into view—three heavy wagons creaking under ore crates, mules lined in rough hemp, and six armed guards walking their span like a cordon. A group of men rode with the merchant in a high-backed buggy—brokers from the mines, a manager from the freight company, and one hard-eyed captain in a gray coat who watched the road the way dogs watch bone. The desert smelled of wet earth and dust. It looked, even to Loren, like the men were grateful for the brief mercy of clean air after weeks of smoke and iron.

Mateo had chosen the place for the ambush with great care—a bend in the road where the wash narrowed, scrub and mesquite on either side, and a tumble of boulders to hide behind. The Rubies had spent the night under the low ribs of a dry arroyo, scent of rain in the air and the wildflowers of spring brushing their boots. Birds called in the mesquite.

Rebecca sat at Loren's side, her hat worn up like a town lady and her pale dress pressed, though there was dust at the hem. Her hair shone like a braid of gold in that pale light. She smiled at Loren, quick and bright, setting him somehow more at ease than all Mateo's plans and John's quiet maps.

"You sure of this?" Loren whispered.

Mateo's voice came back, thin as a thread. "You play. She distracts. Red, Nitis, and Cobb cover the guards with the carts. John grabs the ledger from the merchant while I get the money from buggy. Cobb takes out the buggy driver if it comes to that." He tapped the map once, then folded it away. "Stick to the plan. Quick. Clean."

Rebecca rose when the caravan slowed at the bend. The merchant's lead wagon eased to a halt. As she stepped into the path, Rebecca let her skirts brush the dust and the hem of her dress catch the sunlight. She stumbled—a practiced misstep that sent a ribbon loose. The merchant's men leaned toward the sound like wolves to a cry. Rebecca pressed a hand to her cheek and let out a small, brittle sob.

"Bless the Lord," an old broker muttered, peering through the dust. "Poor soul."

Loren slipped from the brush and onto the road, guitar slung over his back but his voice coming out soft as twilight. He strummed the first chords low, a lullaby in Spanish—with a Creole twist—and the notes flowed like water over men's nerves. The caravan slowed to a stop. The men craned their necks and used this moment to rest their weary legs. Even the hard-eyed captain's shoulders relaxed a beat.

Rebecca moved among them with the ease of a practiced actor. The brush of a gloved hand, a dropped coin, a flutter of lashes. Two guards were close enough that, when she stepped beside them and offered a handkerchief with a smile, John—already in the wagon's shadow—moved right into position without making any broad gestures.

Everything slid into place until it didn't.

One of the merchant's hired guards—a broad-shouldered man missing the tip of his left ear and with a cruel mouth—watched Rebecca too long. He had the menacing look of a man who'd been to border towns and not left with a conscience. He turned from the handkerchief, spat in the dust, and caught sight of movement from the corner of his eye—John sliding the ledger case free. The man's jaw moved, and his hand went to his belt.

"Thief!" he barked.

Rebecca's smile tightened. It was the wrong thing to hear. Every plan depends on the moment a man's attention is where you want it. The shout from the guard pierced the air and, in an instant, the men's attention snapped free from her grasp. The other guards rose, boots grinding in the dirt. The captain barked orders. Two rifles were shouldered. The merchant shouted for the carts to be guided out of the bend.

John cursed under his breath and hastily pulled the ledger from the buggy. "Run it!" he hissed through clenched teeth. Mateo swore and lunged from his hiding place and reached into the wagon floor to grab the sacks of silver coins. Red rose up like a cliff and charged straight in, shotgun barking.

The broad-shouldered guard moved toward Rebecca. He grabbed her wrist as she attempted to spin away.

"No!" Loren's voice broke out sharp and raw. He had not meant to break the rhythm of his song, but he could not listen to the sound of her being hauled off. He had rehearsed keeping men calm with melody a hundred times, but he could not prevent the sudden animal lurch in his chest when danger found the woman for whom he held a strange new tenderness.

Rebecca tried to slide back, to wriggle free, to charm. The guard gripped her wrist like iron and his jaw curled.

"Don't you touch her," Loren roared, and the world became a single, hard line of motion. Loren smacked the guard's arm with his fist. The guard staggered but did not let go.

John—with the ledger under his arm—turned at the other guards, pistol flashing. Mateo was a blade in the wagon, pulling the bags of coin and silver out and piling them onto the dirt. Nitis moved like a shadow, already at the guard's flank, bow bent. Cobb drew and fired.

The first shot ripped through the space between wagons—not at a man but at the dust. Someone reeled and fell, blood spattering the wheels.

The broad-shouldered guard lifted one hand to his hip, to the strap of a pistol. Loren's fingers had trembled at the thought a heartbeat before—no time for breath, only instinct—and he drew as the man swung the butt of his gun toward Rebecca's face.

The report cracked loud as thunder. Loren's bullet found the man's jaw. He lunged forward, hands flailing, and then collapsed into the dirt, eyes glassy. The world slowed—the wound wet and showing a bright ring. Rebecca's hand flew to her mouth as if to stop a scream that would not step out. She stumbled, dizzy.

Another guard—this one shorter, bearded, with a deep scar along his cheek—had started to reach for a knife. John saw him, but he was blocked by the wagon. He cursed and shouted. Loren turned as if on a hinge, the motion fast and clean as a breath. He fired. The second man pitched forward, struck at the neck. Blood spread on the road.

Moments later—flashes, the clatter of bootheels, the howl of a mule—the fight dissolved into a scramble. Mateo and John picked up the bags from the ground. Red and Nitis worked the flanks. Cobb fired wildly, then was hoisted into a saddle and urged away by Red. The merchant's captain, seeing his men felled, drew back, yanked the reins, and screamed for the rest to move. The wagons lurched, wheels tearing up dirt.

The Rubies galloped over the ridge. Horses ripped up the scrub, dust swallowing the sound of dying men. When Loren glanced over his shoulder, he saw Rebecca slumped against the flank of his horse. Her hands covered with dust and trembling.

They slowed when the scrub became thick enough to hide them. The desert closed behind their horse's breaths. The sacks at Mateo's knees thumped with stolen silver.

Red laughed once, high and sharp. "We did it! Glory!"

Cobb's grin was fevered and a little mad. John's jaw was tight like a drawn wire, his hands already weighing out the take. Mateo's eyes shone, hungry and bright. Nitis rode slow... as if his feet were wading through the consequences of men's choices.

Loren's hands shook so hard he could not hold the guitar against his breast. He felt the ringing of his shots in his ears, the thud of men collapsing in the dirt. Rebecca's breath came in small, fragile shudders. He reached for her and felt the tremor in his own grasp.

"You shot them," she said finally, voice thin. Not an accusation, more an astonishment.

"Yes." The single word lodged in him. He had expected to feel triumph, adrenaline, even guilt. Instead came a flat, clinical tiredness, like a man who had run and then stopped and could not find his breath.

John clapped him on the shoulder once, firm. "Quick, clean. No hesitation. That keeps a man alive." The praise was simple, almost mercantile—efficiency over pity.

But as they rode on, Loren's mind did not calm. The yellow, white, and orange wildflowers of spring—brittlebush and poppies—blurred into a smear. He thought of the old boy on a riverbank long ago, of lullabies, of a father's laugh. He thought of the priest in Tubac who had slipped an old guitar into his hands. He thought of the sight of two men collapsing and not moving.

At night, when the camp was small and embers burned low, Nitis dug out a scrap of jerky and passed it to Rebecca without a word. She excitedly accepted it. The Apache's face had no flames in it when he turned to Loren. He simply said, soft as an arrow's whisper, "You are tormented. Why? You chose."

"What choice did I have?" Loren demanded. "He would have…"

"He would have," Nitis agreed, "or he would not. A man does not always have the choice of whether to kill, only whether to carry what killing leaves behind." He tapped the ground with the flat of his knife. "The desert knows what is owed."

Loren turned the phrase over in his mouth like a bitter coin. He had shot because she—someone he cared for—was being hurt. He would tell himself that until the memory of the men's faces faded into the dark. He had wanted to be a troubadour, the man whose song calmed crowds and softened hearts. Instead, his hand had found the gun.

Rebecca slept with her head on Loren's leg that night. The world felt unsteady. Both promise and peril lay on its edge. In the morning Rebecca smiled in a way that made Loren's chest ache—bright and dangerous, and so very human—and he wondered how much of her he could keep, and how much would be used by men like Mateo.

When they rode out toward the ruins of the mission, the Rubies' laughter rose into the air like smoke from a far fire. They were flush with coin and pride. Cobb roared about the taste of tequila and women in Mexico. Red made crude jokes and slapped Loren's back as if trying to knock the shadow from him. Mateo rode with the easy arrogance of a man who sees the world as a ledger. John managed a precise smile, approving of the work that had been done without hesitation. Nitis's eyes, always the measuring point, watched both Loren and Rebecca with the steady patience of a man who knows the land will ask its price later.

Loren did not sleep soundly that first night back at the hideout. He had new songs in his head, but each one had a thin red line running through the chords. He had saved Rebecca. He had killed to save her. That was the truth. He had crossed a river he could not recross, and he would soon have to learn how to walk along its banks carrying the weight of what he had done.

10

Arizona Territory – 1880

Time wore smooth the sharp edges of what Loren had done. The desert rolled on—new trails, new camps, new songs—and somewhere along the way he and Rebecca fell into a kind of restless closeness. Not peace. Never peace. Only two souls circling the same fire—warming and burning each other in equal measure.

The heat between them settled into something steadier, something dangerous. Loren learned the shape of Rebecca's voice in the dark and the weight of her silence in the morning. Their lives folded into the rhythm of the Rubies, and in that long stretch of months after Loren killed in order to save her, the memory of that night did not fade. It deepened—like a scar that refused to heal.

Loren would later think it was Rebecca who planted the first shadow in his heart. She kissed him one night and whispered, "You remind me of someone I once knew. If you had to choose—me, or them—what would it be?" Loren couldn't answer. She laughed then, but the question lingered like smoke. He knew she wanted more than songs and outlaw rides. She desired control, or freedom... or something Loren couldn't name.

The Rubies trusted him—or, at least, Loren believed they did. Mateo spoke to him like a brother. Loren felt a strong sense of loyalty to them, but he was drawn to Rebecca—a yearning he had not felt before. The conflict within him grew.

After a string of ever-more-daring robberies along the Mexican border—from El Paso to Nogales—stories of the Rubies were growing. Wanted posters hung in jails across the territory. Loren's purse and his conscious had grown heavy. A couple years of excitement provided him with enough coin, a woman in his bed, and tales to write a hundred ballads. But it also left him with haunting images and unshakable guilt.

He recalled the words Nitis had shared with him during their first winter. And the memory of Rebecca's kiss was engraved in his mind. He thought about leaving the Rubies, settling in Sonoita where the land was still cheap, maybe buying cattle or starting a small farm.

He shared his idea with Rebecca one night while they sat alone near the campfire. He strummed his guitar while she hummed a melody. "That's a wonderful dream," she remarked. "You should do it."

It wasn't long after—during a meal with his "family" inside the ruined mission—that Loren told the gang of his intention to leave. He told them that the outlaw life wasn't for him. He wanted to live quietly. *Hopefully with Rebecca*, he thought to himself. Mateo got up from the worn table and walked over to embrace Loren. "You'll always be welcome here, *hermano*." The others followed suit—patting his back or clasping his shoulders.

Cobb grunted. "Being a farmer is harder work than being an outlaw."

"And not nearly as rewarding, but there might be some usefulness... for us." Red lightened the mood a bit when he joked about using Loren's not-yet-acquired house as a hideout from the law.

The next day, Loren grabbed his guitar and belongings. He walked across the courtyard toward Nitis, who was feeding Solano pieces of cottonwood bark. He nodded as Loren approached. "The desert always collects on the debt owed. Most men do not get to choose how they pay it. Maybe you will." He reached out his hand to clasp Loren's and placed a small obsidian stone in it—an Apache Tear—a token of good luck.

***

Loren rented a small adobe near the Santa Cruz River. The adobe sat low to the river, its walls the color of dust, its roof patched with mesquite beams and clay. Loren patched cracks with mud, hauled water in buckets, and worked a small square garden beside it. Rows of corn struggled against the dry earth, but beans and squash took root. María, the widow who owned the general store, stopped by often to share seed, advice, or bread still warm from her clay oven.

For a time, Loren let himself imagine the life of a farmer. His hands grew calloused from the hoe, his back sore from bending. The rhythm was simple—water at dawn, mend the fence, tend the crops, and strum the guitar at night.

Rebecca came and went like the wind. Sometimes she arrived with dust on her dress, a mischievous gleam in her eye. Other times, she slipped in silent and weary, lying beside him with little to say. She never stayed long, but her presence lingered after she left—the smell of her hair on his blanket, the sound of her laugh trapped in the rafters.

One afternoon in early summer, she appeared on horseback while Loren was mending a fence. She swung down easy, eyes dancing. "You've gone and turned farmer on me," she teased.

"I dunno 'bout being a farmer," Loren laughed, brushing dirt from his hands. "But a man's gotta eat."

That evening, after chores were done, they saddled their horses and rode along the riverbank. The desert was still in bloom—prickly pear bursting with crimson fruit, mesquite flowers yellow and heavy with bees, poppies scattered like spilled gold across the flats. The river ran low but steady, its banks lined with cottonwoods whispering in the breeze.

Loren breathed it in and let Solano pick a careful trail along the river stones. "Look at this place," he said, gesturing toward the green valley framed by purple ridges in the distance. "A man could raise cattle here. Build a life. There's room for music, and for quiet."

Rebecca's smile was soft but edged. "And when the quiet turns to boredom? When the nights stretch too long and you hear the coyotes howl, will you be content mending fences instead of chasing silver?"

Loren's jaw tightened. "I think so. Peace has a value too. No gun smoke, no blood on the dirt. Just a man's own work, his own home."

"I hope you believe that," Rebecca said, her voice low. "Your heart's too good for the outlaw life, Loren. Too soft for it. But me..." She shook her head, golden hair catching the dying sun. "I don't know if I can live in peace. Not yet. Maybe not ever."

He stared at her, trying to read the truth in her eyes. "But you'd try? For me?"

Rebecca's laugh was quiet, almost sad. "You want me to say it'd be enough. Maybe for you, it is. Maybe it should be for me." She paused and looked around at the calmness surrounding her. "I'd try. For a little while. But sooner or later, I'd hear the sound of coins clinking, see a drunk flash a fat purse, and I'd itch. I don't know how to be anyone but who I am." She touched his cheek then, tenderly. "But you—you could. You could stay here and be whole. Don't lose that."

Her words haunted him as they rode back in silence, the cottonwoods bending in the twilight breeze.

The weeks that followed felt dreamlike. Loren rose with the sun, worked his patch of garden, and spent evenings playing songs for children outside the chapel. Rebecca came sometimes, washing her hands at the well, helping him stack firewood, laughing as she burned tortillas on his cast iron pan. Loren tried more than a few times to convince Rebecca to settle there with him, but she would always smile and say, "Tomorrow." Then she'd slip away without a word, returning weeks later with dust on her boots and stories of taverns and dice.

He tried not to ask where she went, and she tried not to answer.

For a time, he let himself believe. He believed the adobe walls could shelter him from his past. He believed Rebecca might choose the same life he dreamed of. He believed the church bells and the cottonwoods might drown out the call of excitement.

Loren came to realize that the desert is patient, and its voice never fades. It has a way of calling a man back to his true nature—and collecting the debt owed. Loren remembered the churchyard as the place where he first belonged, where music and blood mingled under desert stars. He recalled the laughter and camaraderie that echoed among the ruined walls. He thought often of those memories during the quiet nights along the Santa Cruz River.

So, when Mateo and Rebecca visited the adobe one evening—bringing with them whiskey and promises—he listened intently. "We ride again soon, *hermano*. Another stagecoach carrying silver from the mines in Bisbee is headed to Tucson. The wagon will be heavy—and guarded by fools. One job, fast and clean. We could use an extra man. You don't have to shoot. Just ride with us and earn a share."

Loren's face had already betrayed his thoughts—the excitement of action was calling to him, and Mateo knew it. He picked up his hat from the small table located in the middle of the house and stood up. "We ride out in two days."

Rebecca met his eye—and for a fleeting second, Loren thought he saw a plea there. *Don't come. Stay here.* Then she stood up from the chair next to the tiny cast iron stove and spoke. Her words were direct. "You'll never leave it behind, will you? The blood, the fire. You like it too much."

Loren tried to resist the outlaw life. There were moments he truly enjoyed the peace and solitude, but the lure of excitement and brotherhood had a firm grasp on his soul. Plus, Rebecca was with them... and he wanted her. Soon Loren was back with the Rubies full-time, the churchyard once again his home.

The heist came two days later on the dusty road between Bisbee and Tucson. The stagecoach rattled along, silver locked in its iron belly, four guards riding alongside. At the bend in the trail near Dragoon Pass, Mateo raised his hand and the Rubies struck.

Nitis loosed two arrows in quick succession, dropping the outriders before they could turn their rifles. Red and Cobb rushed the driver, yanking him down while Rebecca's scream—practiced and sharp—froze the guards in their tracks. John was already on the roof, pistol in each hand, moving with the precision of a hawk striking prey.

Loren rode with Mateo, Solano's hooves hammering dust as they surged alongside the coach. Mateo fired once, shattering the lock on the coach door. "Now, *hermano*!" he roared. Loren swung aboard, kicking in the door, gun in hand. Inside, the courier reached for his weapon, but Loren's cold glare was faster.

"Don't," he said simply, and the man froze.

In less than a minute it was done. Silver sacks were slung across saddles, the stage left groaning and empty on the road. No hesitation. Just speed, precision, and the sharp, wild thrill of a clean job.

They rode hard into the hills, laughter carried on the wind, the weight of silver clinking like music in their saddlebags. Red slapped Loren's back with a booming cheer. "That's how it's done, brother!"

Even Cobb, bloodied lip split from the scuffle with the driver, was grinning wide. Mateo rode at the front, a grin stretching from ear to ear. For a few breathless hours, Loren felt the weight of peace slip away entirely, replaced by the old fire—the rhythm of hooves, the bond of men, and a song of outlaw glory.

The small adobe and the tiny garden became both a distant memory and a dream. The brief feel of peace in his hands, only for it to evaporate away like water on the desert sand, never escaped his thoughts. Many nights, while sitting around small campfires with his brothers, strumming on his guitar, he would ask himself, *Did I make the right choice?*

11

Arizona Territory – 1881

The morning air outside the Mormon settlement of Mesa was filled with the smell of alfalfa and cattle—rising from the desert like a stubborn prayer. Straight-lined irrigation ditches carved through the dusty fields, coaxing green from land that didn't want to give it. Whitewashed houses stood in neat rows, shutters closed tight against both heat and gossip. Men worked with heads down, their sleeves rolled to the elbow. Women moved like quiet ghosts between wash buckets and gardens. Children laughed soft, as though joy itself might draw unwanted attention.

Loren watched it all with a strange ache. These were people building toward something—roots, fences, futures. He wondered if there had ever been a version of himself that could have fit inside a town like this. He pulled his hat lower, squinting toward the sun rising over the Superstition Mountains. His face was a little rougher now. The years of riding back and forth across the territory had hardened him—body and mind. He sat high in the saddle, the guitar slung across his back as if he were nothing more than a drifting troubadour. To anyone passing by, he was just another hand, a quiet rider out to try his luck at a mining camp.

Only Loren wasn't out for a quiet, casual ride. He was keeping an eye on a narrow pass through the hills—looking for signs of activity. Specifically, he was watching for a stagecoach from Fort McDowell. To the casual rider, the coach would look like any other passenger carriage crossing the ragged terrain. There would be no military markings or escorts. But it was certainly different, and it was going to be guarded by nonuniformed soldiers—of that, he was certain.

Rebecca had contacts in nearly all the major settlements in the territory—Las Cruces, Tucson, Albuquerque. One such friend from the burgeoning town of Phoenix had messaged her about jewels—opals, garnets, and turquoise—at Fort McDowell that were being transported out of the territory, headed east for New York City. Based on the information, it was a large cache and Mateo was eager to get his hands on it. The tension within the gang was high—like an overly taut string on a guitar.

The jewels were discreetly hidden in a secret compartment within the coach—locked in an iron chest under the driver's bench. If the source was to be trusted, the haul would provide enough money to buy horses, whiskey, rifles, and time. Mateo's orders had been clear—no passengers harmed, no waste of bullets, just take the contents of the chest and run.

The Rubies waited in a dry wash that twisted through a patch of palo verdes, saguaros, and prickly pear. Loren's horse stamped nervously, nostrils flaring at the heat already rising from the earth.

John leaned against his saddle horn, chewing a straw. His voice was as cool as always, but the edge was there. "Stage outta be here by sun high. Driver's punctual, they say. Yankees always are."

"You ever get used to it?" Loren asked quietly.

John rolled the straw in his teeth. "To what?"

"This part. The wait."

A faint smile tugged at the corner of John's mouth. "You don't get used to it. You just learn which parts of yourself to turn off." He tapped the butt of his revolver. "Some men can do it. Some can't. If you can't, you best be fast or you'll end up dead."

Loren swallowed. He didn't yet know which kind of man he was.

Nitis, silent as a shadow, sat a little apart from the rest of the gang, scanning the ridgeline. His long black hair hung down his back, tied with leather. He carried his Winchester across his lap like it was part of his own body, but his bow was slung on the side of his saddle just in case. He never shifted in his saddle. His gaze swept the horizon the way a wolf studied a valley—seeing paths, dangers, exits the others never noticed. There were moments when Loren thought Nitis belonged more to the land than to the men who rode with him. He rarely spoke, but when he did, it was with a weight that settled deep.

A strange chill brushed Loren's spine as he watched him—like the desert itself already knew it would one day reclaim the quiet warrior.

Cobb grinned through a gap-toothed smile. "Easy money, boys. They won't expect, or notice, a couple shadows in the sand."

Loren said nothing. His stomach knotted the way it always did before any work. During moments like these he longed to play his guitar, sing a song to push away the quiet dread, but all he could hear was the desert wind rattling through the palo verdes. Sometimes he wondered if the fear was punishment—a toll exacted for every step he'd taken down this road. Once, he'd sung under bright lanterns for families gathered close and kind. Now the only audience he earned were ghosts and gun barrels. His guitar, slung across his back, felt like a relic from another man's life. The outlaw and the troubadour—two men riding the same horse, pulling the reins in opposite directions. He didn't know which one would win.

Mateo rode down into the wash, his bay horse sure-footed on the rocks. His voice carried command without effort. "Positions. John and Red, you're with me on the road. Cobb, take the ridge. Nitis—cover our backs. Loren..." He fixed him with that hard stare that could slice a man. "You keep any passengers inside the coach calm. You've got the voice for it."

Loren nodded. His voice. His guitar. He wondered how many more robberies he'd be asked to soothe with music.

They set the trap where the stage road narrowed between two rocky bluffs. Fort McDowell lay just ten miles north, its walls—and the soldiers—would be out of reach and too far away to respond. If they could avoid firing their guns, it would be quite some time before the army even knew about the robbery.

The heat thickened. Hours passed slow. A hawk circled high. Loren's shirt clung to his back.

Finally, dust rose on the horizon. The sound came next—the creak of wheels, the jingle of harness.

Mateo raised his hand. Every man tightened his reins.

The stage came into view, drawn by four lathered bays. The driver hunched forward, whip snapping lightly. A guard sat beside him, a scattergun across his knees, eyes sharp under a slouch hat.

Passengers rode inside. Loren counted three faces through the dusty windows—a lady in a bonnet, a thin man in spectacles, and another shadowed figure he couldn't quite make out. *Is that a soldier?* he thought.

Mateo spurred forward. "Now."

The Rubies came down like wolves on a lamb.

John rode straight for the lead team, pistol drawn but steady. Cobb's rifle cracked from the ridge, splintering a branch just ahead of the horses, making them rear and scream.

The stage lurched to a stop. The guard yanked up his gun—but Red's shot knocked the weapon clean from his grip.

"Hands high, *pendejo*!" Mateo barked, revolver leveled.

The driver froze. Dust swirled. The woman screamed, muffled by the stage's walls.

Loren rode forward slow, his hands up as though to calm the very air. "No one has to die here," he said, his voice low, almost gentle. He swung from his horse, boots crunching gravel, and opened the stage door. "Step out, folks. Just a pause in your journey."

The lady trembled, clutching her parasol like a sword. The man with spectacles stammered prayers under his breath. The third passenger stepped down last—sunlight revealed him as a broad-shouldered miner with a cruel jaw, fists clenched as if ready to swing.

"Best keep calm," Loren said softly. "The faster we finish, the sooner you'll be free."

Mateo and John hauled the heavy chest out from under the driver's bench. The thing was heavy, thudding onto the dirt like a dropped anvil.

"Open it," Mateo snapped.

The driver swallowed. "Ain't got the key. It's army-locked."

Mateo grinned, all teeth. "Then we'll take it with us." He jerked his head at Red. "Help John load it."

While the men strained with the chest, the female passenger approached Loren and began slamming her gloved fists into him. She was in his face—and line of sight—when the miner that had also been in the carriage suddenly lunged. He grabbed at Loren, trying to wrestle the pistol from his hand. Loren broke free of the miner's grasp and shoved the miner away. The miner lost his balance and crashed into the lady, knocking her to the ground. The woman shrieked. The horses reared again. The desert exploded in chaos.

"Stand down!" Loren shouted, his boots digging trenches in the dirt. The panic started to rise.

The miner regained his footing and came at Loren again. He swung a fist like a hammer, catching Loren across the cheek. Stars burst behind his eyes. His pistol went skittering across the sandy floor of the trail.

For a moment, Loren thought the man might beat him to the ground. But instinct took over—dark, cold instinct. He yanked the knife from his belt and slashed. The blade caught the miner's arm, blood streaking across his shirt. The man groaned, staggering back, eyes wide with shock more than pain.

Nitis appeared, rifle lowered, his gaze unreadable. He said nothing, but the unspoken threat in his presence was enough. The miner stumbled away, clutching his wound, and sank to his knees in the dirt.

Loren's hand shook. He wanted to vomit. He hadn't killed the man, but the line had been crossed. Again.

The chest was lashed across a packhorse, and the Rubies mounted quick. Mateo fired a warning shot into the air. "Stay put if you want to keep breathing!"

The stage passengers cowered, dust rising around them like smoke. The driver stared at Loren, eyes hard, memorizing his face. Loren turned away. He didn't want to be remembered like this.

The Rubies thundered into the desert, the heavy chest dragging the packhorse into a staggering trot. Behind them, the woman's cries faded into silence.

They camped in the foothills of the San Tan hills, where ocotillo reached like skeletal arms toward the stars. A fire burned low, casting orange across their faces. Cobb drank deep from a flask. "To easy money," he slurred, raising it high.

Loren snorted. "Easy? You didn't have fists in your face."

"This is a big take!" Red cheered as the flask was being passed to him. Mateo watched Loren across the fire. "You held steady," he said flatly. "That's what matters."

But Loren shook his head. "He wasn't armed. Just angry. Maybe scared."

Mateo leaned in, eyes hard. "Fear don't matter. Survival does. You chose right."

The fire popped and hissed. Coyotes yipped somewhere out in the dark. Loren rubbed the bloodstain from his knife until the steel reflected the flames. No matter how long he polished, he could still feel the miner's fear clinging to the blade like oil. The man had only wanted to defend his pride—maybe the woman beside him. Or maybe he'd just been tired of being pushed around by the world.

Loren stared into the coals until they blurred. No ballad would drown out the sound of that woman's scream.

Rebecca appeared on the horizon, riding in from a late trail. She had been kept at distance, near the fort itself. She was on watch for any soldiers that were dispatched for pursuit. "It's clear. They sent out a patrol, but they couldn't pick up the trail," she said as she dismounted. Her skirt caught the firelight creating a curvy silhouette as she walked straight to Loren. Her hand brushed his jaw where the bruise was darkening. "You'll carry that mark awhile," she said softly. "Wear it proud. It means you stood your ground."

Loren didn't answer. He sat staring into the fire, hearing the miner's shout in his ears and tasting the iron tang of blood that wasn't his.

Somewhere deep inside, a voice whispered. *You're not just playing at outlaw anymore. You're becoming one.* And for all his shame, a darker truth rose alongside it. The rush, the heat, the violence, and the escape had made him feel more alive than anything else in his life.

12

Arizona Territory – 1881

The lamps of Tombstone burned bright against the desert night, spilling yellow light onto Allen Street. Horses stamped outside the Bird Cage Theatre, while saloons roared with piano music, dice rattles, and drunken shouts.

The Rubies rode in a tight cluster as they approached the main street, dusty from the trail and hungry for whiskey. It had been a couple months since the robbery near Fort McDowell. Mateo had taken Red with him and sold the jewels to merchants in El Paso. He had instructed the rest of the gang to meet outside Tomb-stone. Mateo's orders were clear—drink, gamble, and spend just enough coin to blend in. Not too much, not too little. Loren and the others knew—Tombstone was the kind of town where outlaws wore badges and carried a long memory.

His cheek no longer ached and his knife was clean, but the weight of the stage robbery was ever present in Loren's mind. He tried to let the noise and smoke of the town drown out the miner's blood still dried on his memory.

The Rubies dismounted, tied their horses to a nearby post, and started walking down Allen Street. The boardwalk creaked under bootheels, lined with polished glass windows that looked out over dust and dung. A church bell tolled somewhere distant, swallowed almost immediately by the clang of a blacksmith's hammer and the hoarse laughter spilling from the Bird Cage. Ladies in silks and bonnets shared the street with drifters in rags, and the air was thick with the mingled scents of cigar smoke, horse sweat, and frying beef.

Mateo let out a low whistle as they passed the Crystal Palace Saloon. "*¡Mira, hermanos!* Town's alive tonight. You can smell the money in the air."

Red spat into the dust. "Or the noose, if we ain't careful."

Mateo stopped outside the Oriental Saloon, the brightest joint on the street. "This one. We'll drink here. Remember—you're ranch hands, trail-weary, nothing more. Keep your mouths clean."

Nitis gave a curt nod, silent as always, then slipped away into the shadows, his task clear—watch their backs.

The saloon was thick with smoke and the sound of a piano clanging some half-forgotten tune. Gamblers packed the faro tables, greenbacks and silver piled high. Girls in feathered hair drifted among the tables, their laughter sharp as spurs.

Loren felt the pull of it—this world of chance, fire, and illusion. For a moment, he wished he were nothing more than a drifting guitarist, free to play for coins and smiles. But he wasn't. He was a Ruby.

The gang took a table in the back, and soon whiskey flowed into small glasses. Cobb raised his drink, voice booming. "To easy money, boys!"

Mateo's hand shot across the table, gripping Cobb's wrist tight. His smile was pleasant, but his eyes were daggers. "Lower your voice, *amigo*." Cobb grunted but quieted.

Loren sipped, letting the fire burn down his throat. Rebecca joined them not long after, slipping in through the side door in a pale-blue dress that clung to her hips. She looked like she belonged in Tombstone, not in some dusty outlaw camp. Her eyes found Loren immediately.

"You don't look like you're having a good time," she teased, sliding into the chair beside him. "I'd give you a penny for your thoughts, but I'm not sure I have enough on me."

"I can't stop thinking 'bout that stage robbery in the Superstitions. Damn stage passenger thought I was his punching bag," Loren muttered. "Why didn't he just stay calm?"

She brushed a lock of hair from her shoulder, whispering so only he heard, "Did you enjoy it?" The question cut too close. Loren stared into his whiskey, saying nothing.

At the faro table, an argument broke out. A local drunk, known around Tombstone as Sam, slammed his fist down—hard—and the cards jumped off the table. "Marked!" he shouted, voice ragged from whiskey. "These cards are marked, damn you!"

The dealer, slick-haired and smiling with too many teeth, raised his palms. "Now hold on. You're just down on luck. Nothin' wrong with the deck but your eyes."

Sam shoved his chair back with a screech. "Luck my ass! I seen you slide that queen from the bottom. Think I don't know a cheat when I see one?"

Other players stirred. One prospector, face leathered from the sun, muttered, "He's got a point, been losin' steady since you came in." Another shook his head, gathering his winnings quick. "No, Sam, you're drunk again. Sit down 'fore you get us all shot."

Sam's hand hovered near his belt. The room tightened around him. The piano player's fingers faltered, then stilled. Dice clattered once and were silent. Even the barmaids froze in place, skirts swaying like flags in a windless hour.

The saloon froze.

Loren felt his throat go dry. His hand strayed toward his pistol, but Mateo caught his wrist under the table. "Not our fight," he hissed.

The standoff ended when the dealer tossed Sam his money back. Laughter rolled through the room, and the piano resumed, though the smoky air stayed sharp with tension.

Rebecca leaned close to Loren. "You see it, don't you? This town's a tinderbox. One spark…"

Sam spat on the floor. "I'll gut you here, you lyin' bastard."

The dealer's smile slipped. He reached under the table. Half the room reached for iron.

Before guns could flash, the dealer threw a stack of greenbacks onto the felt. "Fine! Take it, you crazy son of a bitch! Just sit down before the Earps hear!"

Sam scooped up the money, cursing under his breath, and staggered out into the night. The tension in the bar cracked like a thunderclap. Laughter broke out in nervous gusts.

Rebecca continued to gaze at the faro table. "This place doesn't need much of an excuse," she softly muttered. Her words hung in the smoke like prophecy.

The piano player resumed his clanging, but slower and softer. The air stayed sharp, brittle. The Rubies picked up their glasses and returned to drinking.

It was Cobb who struck the spark.

A cattleman at the bar—broad-shouldered, red-faced, chewing a wad of tobacco—laughed at the Kansas twang in Cobb's voice. "Listen to this hayseed talk, boys. Ain't he the prettiest drunk you ever heard?"

Cobb's face darkened. His fist came like a hammer, slamming into the cattleman's jaw. The man toppled into a table with a crash of glass and whiskey. Instant chaos.

Two of the cattleman's friends lunged from their stools, one grabbing a bottle, the other drawing a knife. Cobb roared and threw himself at them. Chairs toppled, boots scraped, and suddenly the Oriental was a boiling storm.

Loren sprang to his feet, pistol half out of its holster. A barmaid screamed and ducked behind the counter. The piano gave a discordant shriek as the player bolted for cover.

One of the cattlemen swung a chair, splintering it across Cobb's back. Red charged in with a grin, throwing the man into another table. John flipped their own table up, crouching behind it as bullets ripped splinters from the wall.

Loren ducked as glass shattered overhead. A bottle exploded near his head, spraying whiskey down his sleeve. His heart thundered—it was Globe all over again, but louder, closer, hotter. He saw Cobb brawling with two men near the bar, fists and knives flashing. Rebecca was still next to Loren. She had taken cover behind a couple of chairs that had fallen over, her eyes wide but unflinching.

And then Mateo rose. Calm as a priest, furious as a storm. He drew, raised his revolver high, and fired two shots into the ceiling. The boom silenced the room. Plaster snowed down. The smoke of powder hung thick, curling between the lanterns. "¡*Basta*!" Mateo barked. "Enough!" The cattlemen froze, knives still drawn, breathing hard. Mateo's revolver stayed level. His voice carried a weight that silenced even the piano. "Walk away," he growled.

The cattlemen hesitated, then cursed and dragged their bleeding friend toward the door. The saloon exhaled all at once, whispers rising in their wake. One of the bar patrons slurred, "The Earps'll hear 'bout this." Another spat into the sawdust on the floorboards. "Ain't no fight stays quiet in this town."

They were right, the damage had been done. The deputies would hear of this before morning, and the name of Vargas and his Rubies would ripple through Tombstone's veins like fire through brush. Mateo holstered his gun slow, his eyes hard. "Mount up. Now."

The Rubies spilled into the night air, breath steaming in anger and drink. The lamps along Allen Street burned steady, but the mood had shifted. Men leaned on hitching posts, watching. Women in silks peeked from second-story balconies, whispering. Somewhere down the line, a door banged shut.

Cobb wiped blood from his nose and spat. "They had it comin'."

Mateo shoved him hard against a hitching post. "You fool! One wrong word, one wrong move, and the law will sniff us out. You think the Earps don't notice men like us?" At that name, Loren stiffened. Everyone knew the Earps—Wyatt, Virgil, and Morgan—ruled Tombstone with iron hands. Lawmen who lived for the fight as much as any outlaw.

Rebecca stepped between them, her eyes flashing. "Enough. Arguing here only makes you stand out more." Loren knew she was right. Already, heads turned from the Bird Cage. Shadows moved at the end of the street—maybe drunks, maybe deputies.

Mateo growled low but released Cobb. "Mount up. We go to the camp. Tomorrow, we ride for Sonoita until things cool."

And then Loren saw them. Two figures at the far end of the street, standing too still to be drunks. Wide-brimmed hats low, rifles slung casual but ready.

Deputies, no doubt. Behind them, another shape moved out of the Bird Cage's glow—tall, mustached, a badge catching the lamplight.

Cobb stiffened. "Hell. That's Virgil Earp."

Mateo cursed under his breath. "Quiet."

The lawmen didn't approach, not yet. They just watched, eyes like lanterns in the dark. The message was clear to Loren. Tombstone had seen the Rubies, measured them, and would remember.

Rebecca leaned close to Loren, her hand slipping into his for just a moment. "This town eats men alive," she whispered. "Don't give it your name."

Mateo swung into the saddle, his voice cutting low and hard. "Ride. Tonight, we sleep outside this cursed place." The Rubies spurred their mounts and clattered down the street. The lamps of Tombstone receded behind them, but the weight of those steady eyes lingered. Loren knew—the law wasn't just chasing them in the desert. It was waiting, patient, in the very heart of towns like this.

They camped that night outside town, in a dry canyon where the mesquite bent low over the trail. The whiskey wore off, leaving silence and suspicion. Loren sat apart, his guitar finally in his lap. His fingers traced out a slow tune—half lullaby, half lament. The notes drifted like ghosts into the desert night. Rebecca approached, kneeling beside him. Her hand brushed his arm. "You play like a man carrying too much."

He laughed bitterly. "Maybe I am."

"You don't belong to this life," she said softly. "I see it in your eyes. You're kind. Kind men don't last in this world. That scares you more than the guns."

Loren stopped playing. He stared at the stars, fighting the truth in her words. "Yet I'm still here, ain't I?"

Rebecca's hand lingered on his. "For now."

The desert wind carried coyote howls through the dark, sharp and haunting. Loren wondered, as the fire crackled low, whether he'd live long enough to prove her wrong—or die proving her right.

13

Arizona Territory – 1881

The Huachuca Mountains rose like a dark wall against the starlit horizon. Mesquite and oak clustered thick in the canyons, while hidden springs trickled cold water over stone. To Loren, the land felt both beautiful and cruel—the kind of place a man could disappear in.

The Rubies rode in silence that morning, weaving through washes and ridges. Mateo had them keep to narrow trails, away from the stage roads and cattle paths.

Loren's horse picked its way carefully along a rocky incline. His body ached from whiskey and restless sleep, but his mind wandered further still. The events in Tombstone still burned in memory like the echo of gunfire. It had been nearly six months, but Loren could recall all the details... like some haunting ballad he'd sung too many times. He could feel Rebecca's words from that night clinging to him like desert dust. *You don't belong to this life.*

By midday, they reached a canyon mouth thick with sycamore trees. Nitis had scouted it days before—a box canyon with only one way in, and water enough for horses. They dismounted, leading their animals into shade.

"A man could hide here forever. No law, no noise," John said as he stretched out his arms, rolling his shoulders. Red smirked behind his bushy beard. "Yeah, till the Apaches find us."

Nitis gave Red a cold glance but said nothing. He set to gathering brush for a cookfire, his silence more cutting than words. Mateo moved among them like a general, barking orders. "Two men on watch. Cobb, John—you go first. Loren, see to the horses. Rebecca, make the fire. We'll lay low here for a while." They worked in uneasy quiet. Loren looked around at the canyon walls—seemingly pressing down on them, full of secrets and shadows—and shivered.

As he brushed down his horse, Loren's mind slipped backward, unbidden. He saw himself younger, traveling alone across the Sonoran Desert, guitar strapped across his back. He had been no outlaw then, only a drifting hand looking for work. He remembered a ranch outside Benson—the foreman offered him a bunk and a week's pay. For a time, he'd thought maybe he'd found a place to stay. It didn't last. The rancher's daughter had been kind—too kind. Her brothers had seen it, called him a thief of hearts, and one night they'd set on him with knives in the barn. Loren still bore the scar across his ribs. He'd left that ranch before dawn, bloodied but alive. The Rubies found him weeks later in a Nogales cantina, nursing whiskey and bitterness. Mateo had seen something in him then, offered him brotherhood where the world had offered only beatings. And Loren had said yes.

The evening cooled. Smoke from Rebecca's fire curled into the canyon air. She moved with practiced grace, stirring beans in a pot, her blue dress now dulled by trail dust. Loren snapped from his reverie when the smell of food hit his nose.

Cobb drank straight from a bottle, his voice thick. "We outta ride south, straight to Mexico. We got enough money from that jewel heist. Let's go where no law can touch us."

John chuckled at the idea. "And spend it all in a month on tequila and women. No thanks. Mateo has a plan."

All eyes turned to their leader. Mateo leaned against a boulder, the firelight painting his face in harsh lines. "This is only the beginning. We've bloodied our hands. Now we keep them bloody. We are getting rich. We'll buy weapons, horses, safe houses. The Rubies will be more than bandits—we'll be a family with wealth and power."

Loren strummed a low chord on his guitar, feeling uneasy. "A power built on blood don't last long, Mateo."

Mateo's eyes flicked to him, sharp but not angry. "And what do you suggest, *hermano*? Go back to playing for coins on dusty porches?" The fire popped between them.

Rebecca's gaze lingered on Loren, quiet but full of meaning. He couldn't answer Mateo. Not honestly.

When his turn at watch came that night, Loren climbed to a ridge above camp. The moon hung low, silvering the canyon floor. Coyotes yipped in the distance, and somewhere an owl hooted. He settled with his rifle across his lap, but his thoughts wandered again. *Is this all I am? A good man doing bad things? Or a bad man convincing himself otherwise?*

Footsteps approached softly behind him. He turned, finger brushing on the rifle's trigger. It was Rebecca. She carried a blanket around her shoulders, hair loose in the night breeze. She sat beside him without a word, gazing out over the ridges. "Could you walk away?" she asked finally. "If you truly wanted to?"

Loren sighed. "I tried once. But now? I don't know. Mateo brought me in, saved me from fighting this world alone. Red, John... even Nitis. They're my brothers. You don't just turn your back on that."

"And what about turning your back on yourself?" Her voice was soft but cutting.

He said nothing, staring at the moonlight spilling over the rocks. Rebecca's hand brushed his. Just a whisper of touch, but it sent a jolt through him. "You're better than this, Loren. I can see it, even if you can't." She left him with that, slipping back to camp like a shadow.

Loren sat alone for hours, listening to the coyotes, the words echoing in his head like a curse. Toward dawn, when the sun cast a sliver of light across the horizon, he thought he saw a faint metallic glint on a ridge and movement on the far ridge. A flicker, a shadow. His rifle came up, heart hammering.

Nothing. Only rocks and trees. But the feeling stayed with him—that they were being watched.

When Mateo relieved him, Loren hesitated. "I saw something. Maybe riders."

Mateo's eyes narrowed. "Law? Soldiers out of Fort Huachuca?"

"Could be. Or Apaches."

Mateo grunted. "We'll move at first light. Stay sharp."

The Huachucas had hidden the Rubies—for now. But the mountains whispered danger with every breath of wind. And Loren felt it deep in his bones—the ghosts of his past and the weight of his choices were riding hard behind him.

The Rubies broke camp at first light, leaving the canyon in silence except for the brush of hooves over stone. The Huachuca Mountains loomed higher now, shadowed ridges and hidden canyons that could cradle a man for years or swallow him in a single bad turn.

Loren rode second in line behind Mateo, scanning the ridgelines. The feeling of being watched still clung to him like a fever. Every rustle of mesquite, every distant birdcall set his nerves taut.

They wound through a dry arroyo, the smell of dust and horse sweat heavy in the air. The hush was too quiet, even the birds had seemingly gone still. The horses stamped across the gravel uneasily.

"We ain't alone," Loren muttered.

Mateo glanced back. "You think the army's on our trail?"

"I *know* they are. They ain't gonna let it go. The bank job in Silver City or the jewels we stole near Fort McDowell... riled 'em up like a hornets' nest. They'll be coming."

Red spat into the dirt. "Let 'em. I'd like to see their blue coats up close."

Nitis turned his head slowly, his braids falling over his shoulders. "The soldiers bring Gatlings now. Not just rifles." The silence that followed carried more weight than that chest they stole.

By midmorning, they spotted smoke. Thin, rising from the east, no more than a mile off. "Campfire," Red whispered. "Soldiers, maybe."

Mateo studied the smoke. His jaw set. "We swing north. Around the ridge. Keep low."

But the trail they chose was narrow, boxed in by rock walls. It felt like a funnel, leading them into unseen hands. Loren's unease grew. He dismounted, crouching to study the sand. "Fresh tracks. Shod horses. Heavy. A dozen, maybe more."

Rebecca leaned close, her voice tense. "Then we ride the other way."

Mateo shook his head. "No. We ride through. Straight and fast. Surprise is on our side."

Loren felt the old push and pull inside him—the part that wanted to follow and the part screaming that this was madness.

They hadn't gone half a mile when the first shot cracked. A bullet kicked dust at Loren's stirrup.

"AMBUSH!" Nitis roared.

Soldiers rose from behind rocks on both sides of the arroyo, rifles leveled. The air filled with the thunder of carbines. Horses screamed, men shouted.

Red fired wildly, both his teeth and his revolver flashing. John slid from his saddle, rifle in hand, dropping one trooper before a slug hit him in the shoulder.

Loren's instincts took over. He spurred his horse into cover behind a boulder, pistol barking twice. A soldier fell, blood spraying red over the pale stone. Rebecca screamed as her horse reared, nearly throwing her. Loren lunged, grabbing her reins, dragging her to safety.

"Stay with me!" he shouted. She clung to him, eyes wide with terror.

The canyon echoed with chaos. Mateo was everywhere at once, shouting orders, rifle cracking.

Nitis moved like a ghost, bow in hand—he was silent death from the shadows. His arrows flew swift, cutting down two soldiers before they even knew from where the death had come. For a heartbeat, Loren thought the man untouchable, a spirit of the desert itself.

Then came the break in rhythm.

A soldier rose from behind a boulder, rifle leveled at Loren's exposed flank. Loren froze—too slow, too far to draw. But Nitis's voice tore through the canyon like a hawk's cry. "Down!" The bowstring snapped once more, the arrow flying true, punching into the soldier's chest. The man staggered and dropped.

In that same instant, another rifle cracked.

Nitis jerked, the force of the shot throwing him backward into the dust. His bow clattered on stone, string twanging a last mournful note. Loren's eyes locked with his for a split second across the smoke and chaos—steady, unflinching, already fading.

The tide of battle swept on, the soldiers pressed hard, disciplined, driving the gang toward the canyon's narrow opening. Loren fired wildly, heart pounding, but the image of Nitis falling branded itself into his mind like a scar.

"Back! Fall back!" Mateo bellowed.

They cut through the smoke and gunfire, forcing their way toward the canyon mouth. The deafening echo of hooves careening off the canyon walls. Loren fired until his pistols clicked empty, then swung them by the barrels, smashing a trooper's jaw before snatching up the man's dropped rifle.

Beside him, Red whooped like a madman, blood running down his arm. "Ha! Send me more bluebellies!"

As they broke free of the canyon, soldiers gave chase. Cavalry horses thundered after them, sabers flashing in the sun. The Rubies were bleeding. John sagged in the saddle, half conscious. One of their own, Nitis, lay somewhere behind them—in the dust, eyes staring at nothing. A Ruby lost in the desert.

Loren leaned low over his horse's neck. "Ride, damn you, ride!"

They pounded across the desert, the sound of hooves like a thousand drums. The horses' flanks slick with foam, mouths frothing. Bullets hissed past, kicking sand into the air.

One trooper gained on Loren's flank, saber raised. Loren twisted, firing the stolen rifle point-blank. The man toppled backward, his blade spinning away.

The chase stretched on, mile after mile, until finally the Rubies pulled ahead, the cavalry falling back toward Fort Huachuca. The gang didn't slow until the mountains swallowed them again.

They sheltered in a limestone cave high above a dry wash, the horses lathered and trembling. Gunpowder still stinging the throat, and the metallic tang of blood mixing with sweat.

John groaned as Rebecca pressed cloth to his wound.

Cobb sat against the wall, laughing through clenched teeth, his face pale. "We did it. We whipped the bastards."

Loren rounded on him. "We didn't whip 'em. We barely made it out. One of us didn't. We're hunted now, worse than before."

It was then he noticed it. Against the wall, near the scattered saddlebags and rifles—Nitis's bow. Someone had grabbed it in the scramble from the canyon. The wood was dark with desert dust, the string frayed, useless now without the man who had drawn it. The sight of it cut deeper than any wound. Silent, accusing, it was an unspoken gravestone laid among them. A reminder of what will come.

Mateo wiped blood from his cheek. His eyes burned with fury, not fear. "Good. Let them hunt. Every bullet they spend on us is one they don't fire at others. We'll make the name *Rubies* one the army curses."

Loren stared at him. "And what of the rest of us? How many brothers do we bury before you're satisfied?"

The cave went quiet. The only sound was John's labored breathing. In the corner—partially hidden in shadow—the bow. Rebecca met Loren's eyes across the firelight. There was fear there but something else too. A plea. *Leave this life. Before it takes you too.*

When his watch came, Loren stepped outside into the cool mountain air. The stars spread above him, endless and sharp. He thought of his first days in the territory—his guitar, the promise of music and quiet living. How far he'd fallen from that man. And yet, when he closed his eyes, he still felt the rush of the fight—the blood, the fire, the bond of men at his side.

He hated it. He craved it. A good man doing bad things, or a bad man convincing himself otherwise?

Behind him, the gang slept fitful in the cave. The bow lay among their things, mute and heavy as a coffin lid. Ahead lay more blood, more law, more running. And somewhere, Loren knew, the gallows waited.

14

Arizona Territory – 1881

The ruins of the old mission lay quiet under the summer sun, its crumbling walls casting long shadows across the courtyard. Mesquite and creosote whispered in the hot breeze, and the faint ring of Loren's guitar carried through the air like a prayer for a place too forgotten to care.

They had been lying low for weeks now, living off the spoils from the jewel heist. The army ambush in the Huachucas was growing more distant with each passing day. The law had gone quiet, but Loren knew Mateo would remain cautious. He'd spent too many years in this land to mistake silence for safety.

That evening, the Rubies sat in the shade of the bell tower. Rebecca poured whiskey into chipped tin cups, her golden hair catching what little light still lingered. Red leaned back against the wall, boots crossed, watching the horizon with half-closed eyes. John shuffled a worn deck of cards but didn't deal. The mood looked easy enough—whiskey, shade, the lazy quiet of evening—but Loren could feel something tighter underneath it... like a pulled thread no one mentioned.

Cobb broke the silence.

"We're wastin' time here," he grumbled, lifting his cup. "Coin's meant to be spent. We outta ride south, hit a payroll, a coach—somethin'. Towns are fat with money, and we're sittin' here like chickens in the dirt."

Mateo's laugh was low, without warmth. "And where'd your money go last time you rode south? I recall women, tequila... and not much else."

Cobb's jaw tightened. "Better spent than rottin' away in a sack under the dirt." He looked around at the others. "Tell me I'm wrong. Tell me you ain't itching for more."

Red sat forward, his broad frame blotting the light. "You're wrong. We just buried Nitis. You want to throw the rest of us in the ground chasin' coin we don't need?"

John flicked the deck of cards onto the table between them. "Mateo leads this crew. Always has. If you don't like it, ride on."

Cobb's eyes narrowed, drifting from face to face, searching for some sign of wavering. He found none. Rebecca's gaze was steady, Loren's unreadable, and Red stood firm with Mateo.

Rebecca moved in closer to Loren, her voice a silk thread meant only for him. "He's not wrong, you know. You're restless too. Don't lie to yourself." Her hand lingered on his knee, warm and persuasive. "But you could choose a different kind of restless. Away from all this."

Loren met her eyes, and for a heartbeat the desert seemed to vanish—just her laugh, her breath, and the promise of another life. A quiet life. His chest ached with the thought of it.

The silence stretched until Cobb barked out a bitter laugh. "So that's it. All lined up behind the big man." He slapped the dust from his hat, then stood. "Fine. I'll ride my own trail." Loren could see that Cobb wasn't asking—or waiting—for any blessing. He swung into his saddle without another word. The sound of hooves echoed through the mission yard, fading into the desert until there was nothing left but wind. The Rubies watched him go. No one followed.

When the silence settled again, Red let out a long breath. "Man's got fire but no compass. He'll burn himself out."

Loren strummed a soft chord, his eyes lingering on the empty gate where Cobb had passed. "Or burn someone else with him."

Rebecca leaned into him then, her voice just above the whisper of the wind. "Doesn't have to be your fire, Loren. You could still walk away. I might even come with you."

He didn't answer. The desert night was falling, stars beginning to pierce the sky, and he played on—low and steady—as if the music alone could hold the gang together. But the mission felt emptier now, and Loren knew a fracture had begun.

That night the others slept heavy, but Loren found Mateo still awake, sitting alone beneath the broken archway where the bell once hung. The desert wind moved through the stones like a tired hymn. Mateo cradled a tin cup in both hands, untouched whiskey inside.

"Couldn't sleep?" Loren asked.

Mateo didn't look at him. "When a man like Nitis dies... the world should shake," he said softly. "But it doesn't. Dust blows. Coyotes howl. Men keep riding. Like he was never here at all."

They sat a long while without speaking.

"He saved my life once near Santa Cruz," Mateo said finally. "Arrow in a Mescalero's bow had my name on it. Nitis shot first. Never said a word about it. Just nodded. That was his way."

Loren swallowed. "I keep thinking he'll walk in from the dark."

Mateo's voice roughened. "He won't."

The admission landed like a stone in Loren's chest. Mateo wiped his eyes with the back of his hand—quick, ashamed—then hardened again. "So, we remember him," Mateo said. "We ride smarter. We live longer. Otherwise, he died for fools."

Loren nodded, but the truth sat bitter in his throat. He wasn't sure he was done being a fool.

***

The weeks that followed dragged slow, stretched thin as the desert horizon. The Rubies mended tack, oiled guns, patched clothes, and nursed wounds old and new.

The mission seemed to breathe with them, its walls holding the echo of laughter and gunfire both.

One evening, Loren and Red walked the ruins, their boots crunching in gravel where parishioners once prayed. The sun bled red through the broken bell tower.

"Wish I'd heeded Nitis more," Loren whispered.

Red shook his head. "He knew."

"How?"

Red smiled sadly. "Because you stayed."

"You think Cobb'll be back?" Loren asked.

Red scratched his beard, sighing. "He's like a moth. Always flutterin'. Maybe he's in Mexico, maybe worse. But he don't land long anywhere." He clapped Loren's shoulder. "Don't let his fire pull you in. You burn bright enough already." Loren forced a smile, but his heart twisted. *Bright enough to shine, or bright enough to burn out?*

He walked across the once-sacred grounds and into the old church. In the flicker of lamplight, he sat down at the wooden table in the middle of the room with John, who was cleaning pistols. John's hands were methodical, reverent almost, each screw and spring treated like holy relics. "You ever think about layin' those down?" Loren asked.

John didn't look up. "The guns?"

"Yeah."

"Death has a way of followin' men like us," he murmured.

Loren didn't answer—he feared John was right.

John slid the cleaned cylinder back into place and clicked it shut. "A man lays it down when the world lets him. World ain't let me yet." He handed the revolver to Loren, grip first. "But if you're gonna keep carryin', then carry it right. Skill keeps you alive. Sloppiness gets you buried."

Loren nodded, the weight of the iron heavy in his hand. Music felt lighter.

The next night, Mateo joined Loren near the crumbling altar where he strummed quietly. For a while, Mateo just listened. Then, "What do you think comes next, *hermano*?"

Loren shrugged. "Don't know. Cobb's right, I guess. I get restless. But maybe Rebecca's right too. Maybe peace ain't so bad."

Mateo's laugh was sharp, not cruel but certain. "Peace is for men with fences and sons. You and me... we long for a different kind of piece, eh? We were made for fire. Don't forget that."

Loren strummed one last chord, staring at the dust rising in the moonlight. "What if I don't want fire anymore?"

Mateo's hand clapped Loren's shoulder, heavy as stone. "The fire will still find you."

Loren said nothing. His guitar hung quiet across his knees, caught between song and silence.

Later that week, after night had settled over the mission and the last light faded from the sky until only the stars remained, Loren slipped into the old church with his guitar slung across his shoulder. The others had drifted off to sleep or whiskey, their voices thinning into silence.

Moonlight poured through the gaps in the roof, laying pale stripes across the cracked adobe floor. The altar was long gone. Only a scar in the stone marked where it had once been.

He sat there anyway.

He laid his hat beside him and rested the guitar across his knee. For a long while, he didn't play—he only listened. The desert wind moved through the broken doorway like a breath. Somewhere, a night bird called. The world seemed wide and empty and watching.

Then he strummed—more to himself than to the night. Not loud. Not for show. Just enough for the chords to rise and circle the rafters that were no longer there. A hymn his mother used to hum. Notes full of dust and memory. The sound felt wrong and right all at once—sacred in a place where men like him had no right to kneel.

He closed his eyes. For a heartbeat, he wasn't an outlaw. He wasn't Mateo's "*hermano*" or Rebecca's lover or the man whose pistol spoke too fast. He was a boy again beside a laughing river, fingers stumbling through a song, dreaming of fame or salvation... anything clean.

The music softened.

Boot steps whispered behind him. John stood in the doorway, hat in hand, saying nothing. He listened for a verse or two, then gave a small nod—approval without blessing—and vanished back into the dark.

Loren kept playing. The melody turned somber. Something confessional threaded through it, as if the battered walls might absorb his sins and leave him lighter. But when the final chord faded, the church stayed broken. The desert stayed hungry. And the weight on his chest remained.

He laid the guitar across his lap and whispered into the emptiness, "I don't know which man I am anymore." The night gave no answer. Only the wind. Only the stars. Only the quiet echo of a troubadour who had lost his way.

Rebecca appeared out of the shadows, her dress loose, her hair unbound. She moved with the kind of ease that made the ruins feel like a stage she owned. "You'll wear those strings thin," she teased, settling beside him.

"Strings are cheaper to mend than souls," he answered, fingers trailing over the frets.

She laughed low, then grew quiet, watching his hands. After a long silence, she asked, "What if you could put all this down? The guns, the blood, the running. Just keep the guitar."

Loren shook his head. "Doesn't work that way. Men like me don't get to just lay it all aside."

Rebecca leaned in, her voice soft as the desert wind. "Maybe you're wrong. Maybe you should try again. Find a place out there—small house, bit of land, river close by. You'd work the soil when the sun rose, play songs in the evening. Children running underfoot, your woman waiting on the porch."

Her words drew pictures in his mind so vivid it hurt. He could almost hear the sound of laughter, the smell of tilled earth, the creak of a rocking chair in twilight. "And that woman?" he asked. "Would she stay with a man who's done what I've done?"

Her smile flickered warm and sharp all at once, but her eyes echoed a loneliness that didn't belong to the woman she played. She had the look of someone who had loved once—and paid dearly for it. "Depends on the man he chooses to be. Maybe she'd take the gamble." She let her hand brush his and linger there a moment before pulling away. "Think on it, troubadour."

She rose, slipping back into the dark, leaving Loren with nothing but the echo of her words and the weight of his guitar. He sat a long time, torn clean in two—half yearning for the picture she painted, half knowing the desert would never let him have it.

15

Arizona Territory – 1882

The monsoon rains had moved on by midmorning and the desert wind carried the tang of chaparral as the Rubies rode south from the decayed mission, the sun sinking toward the ragged hills that marked the border. Nogales shimmered in the distance—a sprawl of adobe houses and cantinas pressed against the line of Mexico. Smuggling jobs were nothing new to the Rubies, but tonight Loren felt a tightness running through the family—a kind of quiet unease he couldn't shake.

Loren felt it in the set of the horses' ears, in the silence between the riders. Red had a somber look on his face—no jokes today. John seemed to be riding a little taller than usual. Loren guessed it was his way of reminding the others of his steadiness. Mateo, as always, led with iron purpose, his eyes fixed on the horizon.

"What's the haul this time?" Loren asked, riding up beside him.

"Rifles," Mateo said. "Men across the line will pay well for them when we bring 'em back. And we can keep some for our own purposes."

"And our cut?" Red pressed from behind.

Mateo's mouth tightened. "Enough to keep bellies full and guns loaded."

Loren's gut twisted. He'd learned by now that Mateo rarely answered straight unless he didn't like the truth.

Once in Nogales, they were to meet their contact—Cobb—in a cantina on the Mexican side of the border town. It had been nearly three months since Cobb had ridden off from the gang. Loren had seen him come and go a few times before—Cobb would ride off on his own, only to return when he was cashed out. What he did or where he went was never known... he'd just show back up at the old mission like he'd only been gone for a few nights.

When he rode up to the mission a week ago, he went straight to Mateo about an easy job with a large payout. "A wagonload of rifles. Real simple. I thought about hiring a few guns to help me pull it off, but I thought I'd cut you guys in instead," he said.

"What's your take?" Mateo asked.

"Everythin's been handled. I fronted the coin for the guns, so I want my money back plus a small fee for setting this up," Cobb replied. "Whatever you sell 'em for is all yours."

Mateo thought everything sounded good and with a pat on Cobb's back said, "I knew you'd come home, *amigo.*"

Loren thought it sounded too good to be true.

The cantina on the Mexican side was thick with smoke and guitar music, laughter spilling from shadowed booths. Rebecca slipped through the crowd beside Loren, her shawl pulled close. He'd seen the way her jaw tightened at meetings like this, but Mateo insisted she come. Her presence softened the gang's edge, made them look less like wolves in a pack.

Cobb was leaning against the bar, a half-empty glass in hand. His grin was wide. "Evening, boys." His voice was smooth as oil. "Shipment's ready in the alley." He pointed to the rear of the cantina.

Mateo's eyes narrowed. "Seems too easy." Cobb shrugged. "Business is easy, if you've got the right friends."

Loren studied him, bile rising in his throat. Cobb's boots were too clean for a man running jobs. His eyes darted just a little too much. Loren's hand drifted near his pistol.

Mateo patted Cobb on the shoulder with warmth and grinned. Then he motioned toward the rear door. The Rubies went outside. They stepped into the darkness of the alley that ran between shops. The alley stank of garbage and mule piss. Crates were stacked against the walls. Shadows pooled in every corner. A few buildings down, a small cart with a mule stood waiting—parked halfway into the darkness. They walked over to the cart. The rifles were wrapped in burlap as promised. Everything was ready to go.

Loren's skin prickled. He couldn't shake the feeling of eyes on them.

Then came the whistle. Sharp. Too sharp. Shadows moved on the rooftops. Rifles leveled. Voices shouted in Spanish, "¡*Alto, federales*!" Gunfire erupted and thundered in the narrow street.

Mateo dove for cover. *"El diablo!"* A curse Loren knew was meant for Cobb.

Bullets tore through crates, splinters flying. Red went down to one knee, blasting his shotgun skyward, scattering men on the tiles. John drew both pistols in one motion and fired, dropping a rifleman who had Loren in his sights.

"Son' bitch set us up!" Loren roared.

Rebecca screamed as a slug ripped past her head, tearing a hole in the shawl. Loren threw himself at her, knocking her to the ground, his body shielding hers as plaster dust rained down. "You alright?" he panted. She nodded shakily. "Stay down." He pressed his revolver into her hands. "If anyone comes close, you shoot."

They fought like cornered wolves—desperate and close-quartered. They couldn't go back out the way they came in. The door they came through from the cantina was a furnace of bullets. Their only hope lay ahead—searching for an exit in the labyrinth of dark passageways between the buildings.

Using the crates for cover, the gang battled their way through the alley. Gunfire echoed from every angle. The shots cracked so close the air felt hot. Splinters sprayed with every hit. "¡*Alto*!" echoed off the walls.

Mateo barked orders, urging them forward. "Move!" Red blasted a path with the roar of his shotgun, while John covered their flank, firing with icy precision. The rest of the gang crab-stepped along crooked walls of crates, firing blindly at the muzzle flashes that stitched the dark.

They reached a corner. A breath to look. Another dark alley, another kill zone. Soldiers poured in from all sides, their uniforms flashing under the moonlight. The alley rang with the sound of metal, the slap of boots, the clatter of brass casings. A bayonet licked the corner. Red smashed it aside with the stock of the shotgun and moved into the narrow passage. The others close behind.

They reached the end of the alley and burst onto the main street. A hanging lantern swung mad in the night wind and threw their shadows long and wild. Horses screamed. Civilians fled into doorways. A bell tolled somewhere high. A window blew out and glass pattered the cobble street. A door slammed from a nearby building and a woman wailed and went silent. The Rubies ran low, tight as a pack, each breath a rasp.

They ran to the hitching post for their horses. Each strobe of light from a rooftop muzzle was another bead of their lives. Bullets chewed signs. A rooftop tile broke near Loren's head. He didn't turn. Red whooped like a madman, his scattergun clearing the way. Each recoil slammed his shoulder. And when the shotgun ran dry, he swung it like a club. A soldier in front of him folded and another tripped over him.

"North! To the line!" Mateo shouted above the chaos, pointing between two wagons where the street fell away toward the wash.

They hit the post hard. The animals dancing, their eyes wide. The knot on the lead rope of John's horse was stuck. "Cut it!" Red said. Mateo—always quick with a blade—got his knife on it and sawed through the tarred hemp.

Loren grabbed Rebecca by the wrist and lifted her into the saddle. The horse bunched under them, hot and slick with panic. His arm locked tight around her waist as they galloped toward freedom.

Shouts rose from both ends of the streets. The federales were closing in, saber edges flashing. *"¡Cierren la calle!"* Boots hammered on the stone. A bugle cried thin and far. A barricade at the town's edge rose out of the smoke—a makeshift wall of barrels and a wagon turned on its side. Mateo spotted a gap in the barrier.

"There!" He pointed at the small opening. The gang charged ahead.

A soldier lunged from the shadows and hooked Rebecca's torn shawl. The fabric snapped tight across her throat. Choking, she clawed at the garment noose around her neck. She was nearly pulled from the horse when Loren leaned out of the saddle and fired from the hip. The soldier spun away in a spray of blood, releasing the shawl. Rebecca gasped. Her hands found Loren's shirt and clung. Her face pressed into his chest. He could feel her shaking. "Hold on," he said into her hair. "I've got you."

Behind them, John's horse shrieked. Loren turned just in time to see it collapse, a bullet tearing its hind leg. John hit the ground hard, the weight of the beast pinning him. He raised one pistol, fired three shots in quick succession—saving Red from a shot at his back. Then the federales closed in. "Go!" John shouted, his voice raw. "Ride!" Loren's heart ripped in two as the night swallowed his brother's gunfire.

Unaware that John had fallen, Red slapped his horse and took the gap in the barricade at an angle. Wheels spun. Hooves struck wood. The wagon lurched and slid just enough. A barrel burst and stank of kerosene. The Rubies crashed through—bodies low, knees tight.

The cobble street dropped and became bedrock and sand. They hit the dry wash that cut the border. Hooves drummed the hardpan. Pebbles spat. Rifle fire chased them from behind—snapping past their ears with a wasp's sting. A round ricocheted off a rock. The federales came to the bank and stopped, their breath ghosting in the moonlight. They did not cross.

The climb out of the wash was a scramble. Horses lunged and slid. Nogales fell away behind them. Still shouting, still bright in ugly pulses. The Rubies—their faces streaked with dust and sweat—didn't look back until the first low hill took them out of range and the only sound left was their own breath.

They pulled up among scrub and stone and let the horses rest. Chests heaved. Throats burned. Red checked his shells with hands that didn't feel like his own. Red spat into the dirt. "Cobb's dead meat if I see him again."

Loren only shook his head. "He'll hide well. Men like that always do." His voice was thick, heavy. He felt Rebecca's fingers loosen, one by one, from his shirt. He dismounted from Solano and helped her off the saddle.

Below them, Nogales threw up a smear of smoke and the like—an echo of what they had just been through. Above them, the sky was clean and star raked. Mateo leaned on his saddle horn and listened to the wind for a count of ten. He then wiped blood from his sleeve, his eyes burning with cold fury. His jaw clenched as he scanned the survivors. "Where's Juanito?"

The silence answered for them.

Mateo's face hardened, eyes like flint. "Remember this night," he said, voice low and grim. "This is what betrayal looks like. It nearly cost us all. Loyalty"—he jabbed a finger at his chest—"is all we've got. Without it, we're dead men."

The men nodded in agreement. Loren's gaze drifted to Rebecca. She sat apart from the others, perched on a rock, clutching the torn shawl to her chest. In the starlight her face looked almost hollow. The spark he was used to seeing in her eyes was gone.

Loren looked down at his worn and dusty boots. A thought slowly crept into his head. *How much more can we lose before there's nothing left of us at all?*

16

Arizona Territory – 1882

The mission lay hushed beneath the morning sun when Loren stepped outside. The ruined walls still held the night inside them, shadows clinging like they didn't want to leave. Smoke from last night's fire curled in the courtyard, where boots and saddles sat abandoned in a sprawl of weariness. Somewhere a horse stamped. Somewhere, someone coughed in their sleep. Otherwise, it was quiet.

Loren stepped into the refectory. The long table was littered with empty cups and a few loose cartridges. And there, at the center, lay John's deck of cards. Neat. Squared. Waiting for hands that would never return.

He stopped—not like a man hitting a wall but more like a man coming home to find the house empty. For a long time, Loren only stared, the silence around him louder than gunfire. His throat tightened. He reached out, then drew back, afraid the cards might scatter like the rest of his life.

Rebecca's voice drifted from the doorway, soft as a sigh. "He always did hate leaving a game unfinished."

John was gone. Nitis too. For Loren, the Rubies had bled into ghosts, and the spaces where men should have been felt heavier than the men themselves ever had. Even Mateo's voice—always full of plans and fire—seemed distant now. Loren rested a hand on the back of a chair and let the weight of it hold him up. He'd always told himself that the Rubies were family, but families weren't supposed to vanish one at a time into the dust.

"*You don't belong to this life*," Rebecca had once told him. Standing there in the empty room, he wondered if the life was already letting him go.

That night, while the others drank themselves numb, Loren packed his guitar, a few cartridges, and what coin he had. Rebecca lingered in the shadows of the courtyard, her shawl wrapped tight. She didn't stop him. She only said, "You'll never outrun yourself, Loren."

He left before dawn. The desert stretched wide under him, a quilt of red stone where the horizon bent into heat and silence. Dust rose from Solano's hooves and drifted off behind him. The mesquite trees bent in the wind, whispering secrets he couldn't quite hear. Sometimes a hawk watched from a crooked saguaro, its sharp eyes following him the way debt follows a man. The farther he rode, the more the world emptied, until it felt like only the sky and his guilt were big enough to travel beside him.

Loren was alone now—the Rubies left behind and their faces flickering through his memory like ghosts. Red, full of life and ready to protect it. Nitis, silent and steady, swallowed in dust. John, his cards forever left on the mission table. Cobb's betrayal. Even Mateo, brother and commander, his fire growing too hot to stand near.

He had slipped away without a word. No drawn out "goodbye," no adobe house, no garden this time. Just his guitar, his horse, and the cold steel of his revolver.

***

He drifted across the southern edge of Arizona into Sonora, and farther still, into Chihuahua. Sometimes the road gave him nothing but sky and cactus and the long patience of the desert. He rode through stretches where the land rolled out in shades of copper and bone, the saguaros standing like sentries. In some towns, no one asked his name. In others, they asked too many questions and he rode on before sundown. Dogs barked at him. Old men watched him from porches with the same suspicion he carried in his own bones. He slept where he could—under wagon frames, beside dry creek beds, in the lofts of barns when luck was kind. Most mornings he woke with the same thought pressing on his ribs—*keep moving.*

In cantinas and saloons, he played songs older than the land—haunting *corridos*, ballads of lost loves, and tunes quick enough to set boots stomping. Patrons threw coins onto tables, sometimes a silver peso, sometimes nothing at all but the nod of a drunk with tears in his eyes. Loren played anyway. Each note carried a piece of his wandering soul, each melody both a confession and a prayer.

The music alone never filled his purse. On nights when whiskey blurred the crowd or when laughter grew too loud, Loren's hand worked faster than his song—slipping a coin purse, drawing a pistol to silence a cheat, lifting a small chest from a merchant too fat to notice. Sometimes he caught the way men looked at him—the nods, the lowered voices. As if he were becoming a story men whispered about at campfires and gambling tables along the border.

One night, Loren lay beneath a stand of ironwood trees—saddle for a pillow and his guitar beside him like an old friend. His thoughts turned to the Rubies while the desert cooled and the branches whispered overhead. He felt worn thin. Sleep came slow... and when it came, it did not come gently.

Loren was running. Faces blurred—soldiers, towns-folk, ghosts he half knew. The buildings closed in on each side. Gunfire cracked like thunder, faceless soldiers pouring from the shadows. John's voice cut through the smoke, "Loren! Behind you!" A horse screamed. Loren turned. The street twisted like a serpent coiling around him.

John alone stood in the dust, his back to Loren, guns drawn, calm as always—until a bullet tore through his chest and he folded without a sound. Loren tried to run to him, but the ground turned to mud. His boots sank. His legs would not move. He clawed at the earth as it swallowed him. A hand reached down—Nitis. Loren grasped it.

Suddenly, he was sitting at a table. John sat across from him now, shuffling cards with blood-slick hands. His face expressionless and cold. "Deal you in, partner?" The cards became bullets as they left John's hand. Each one struck Loren in the chest—hot and burning—yet he did not drop, did not bleed. Loren was unable to die.

Then Rebecca stepped from the dark with a torn shawl and empty eyes. She held a golden revolver in her hand—already smoking. She raised the gun. The muzzle rose and grew bigger until it was all Loren could see. "This is what love costs." Her voice echoed inside the barrel. The gun roared.

Loren jerked awake, heart pounding, hand clawing for his Colt. The desert around him lay silent—only the wind in the branches and the faint scrape of insects. His breath came hard. His ribs burned where the bullets should have been. He pressed a hand to his chest, as if he might hold himself together.

He sat a long while, staring into the dark where the dream had been. His throat tightened. The words came out rough and barely louder than breath. "John... I'm sorry." He was sorry for leaving John behind. Sorry for living. Sorry for not being the man John believed he might be. His eyes stung. "And... thank you," he added, as if the dead could hear gratitude any better than regret.

The wind moved through the ironwood leaves like a whisper. Loren bowed his head. "What am I turning into?" he murmured to the empty land. Dawn crept slow across the sky, and Loren knew. *Some ghosts don't ride off.... They travel with you.*

***

On the outskirts of Tucson, he played his guitar in a tiny saloon thick with mezcal smoke. The crowd swayed, clapped, and tossed coins at his feet. Later, he slipped through the back room, lifting a strongbox while the owner slept. By morning, he was gone, leaving half the silver at the steps of the church. He told himself he was balancing the scales. It felt more like rearranging the weight.

In a mining camp near Bisbee, Loren found work for a week playing each evening in a low-roofed cantina where the lamps smoked and the floorboards creaked like tired bones. The men who came there were worn thin by the mountains—faces carved with dust and hunger. He sang ballads of women who waited and didn't, of men who rode out and never came home. Sometimes the room fell so quiet he could hear the glasses settle on the bar at the end of each verse. Other times the music loosened their tongues, and they pounded the tables, laughing like boys. They had little coin to spare for the troubadour who filled their spirits. Loren played for them anyway.

A little girl—the owner's daughter—would sit cross-legged in the corner each night, chin in her hands, watching his fingers dance across the strings. When he finished, she always clapped first. "Play the river song," she'd beg. He always did.

The end of the week brought less coin than he'd hoped. The miners drank on credit, the owner paid late, and Loren's purse felt as hollow as his ribs. He told himself he would ride on in the morning.

That night, after closing, he walked past the office door and saw the cashbox sitting open on the desk—gold and silver coins stacked neat as prayers. He thought of the little girl, of her bare feet on the dusty floor. *Don't*, something in him whispered, but the hunger in his gut—and the sound of the trail calling—drowned it out.

He took only a portion—enough to buy feed for his horse and enough for food for him. Nothing that would ruin the owner and his family. He told himself it wouldn't hurt them much. That lie went down smoother than the whiskey... but it burned longer.

Loren felt like a wandering spirit taken by the Sonoran Desert. The days melted into one another. Sometimes the rain found him—sudden desert rains that came all at once like a confession. The sky would bruise purple, then split open, and the world turned silver and wet. The sand darkened. The creosote woke and filled the air with its clean, sweet breath. Loren never hurried for shelter. He would sit the saddle and let the water run down his face and hands, feeling—just for a moment—as if the dust of every sin might rinse free. But the clouds always moved on. The silence always returned. And the dust still clung to him.

17

Mexico/New Mexico – 1883

Seasons turned like verses in a song. Winter rains filled the washes, and Loren huddled beneath mesquite, plucking low notes while water drummed the tin roof of some forgotten shed. In the quiet between thunder, he wondered whether the storm washed men clean, or only made the dirt settle deeper.

Spring brought wildflowers that burned bright against the dust like stubborn prayers. Summer baked the land hard and long, and Loren learned the taste of sand on his teeth again. By autumn, the skies burned copper and red, and shadows stretched across the ground like roads he had not taken. He drifted on, the borderlands stretching out before him like a song with no end.

In San Miguelito, he sang *corridos* until midnight, his voice weaving tales of riders, gunmen, and lost loves. When two vaqueros tried to drag him outside for cheating at cards, he calmly outdrew them both—a skill honed from the many long days at the mission with John—but fired into the dirt at their feet, laughing as they fled.

He stopped to play songs at the Mormon settlement in Chihuahua. When he finished, some of the children began chasing him around the village square. He reveled in the laughter of the children as they played. One small boy tugged at Loren's sleeve and asked if the pistol on his hip was heavy and if that was why he couldn't outrun them. Loren laughed. Maybe the boy was right.

While passing through a small railway stop along the border, he made off with the cashbox from a mercantile shop after distracting the shopkeeper's daughter. He gave a fistful of coins to a widow and slipped the rest into his guitar case. By nightfall, he was on the road again, horse hooves drumming against the dust.

***

South of El Paso, the land turned to dust and thorn. Mesquite hunched low over the earth like old men guarding secrets, and the wind carried grit that scoured the teeth. Loren rode into a pueblo that seemed half erased by the desert with its sun-bleached adobes, a cracked well, and a shrine to the Virgin tucked into a wall where candles burned low and steady.

He stayed. One night. Then another. The cantina owner paid him in beans, bread, and a cot at the back. Word spread quick when a guitar came to town. By the third evening the room was full with miners, ranch hands, women with tired smiles and bright scarves, and children peeking in from the doorway. Loren played melodies soft enough to let the night breathe. Coins clinked into a chipped cup. Someone laughed for the first time in weeks.

That was when the bandits rode in. Five of them. Dust-coated. Spurs jangling sharp as broken glass. They pushed through the cantina doors like they owned the earth beneath their boots. The leader wore a blue caval-ry coat with the brass buttons polished bright, a trophy torn from some other man's life. They didn't bother to order drinks.

One slammed a man's head into the bar. Another tore the earrings from a woman's ears while she cried out. A third knocked the cantina boy to the floor and kicked him twice for moving too slow. They took rings, watches, and whatever silver the poor could not spare. The air turned mean.

Loren's eyes filled with anger and disgust, but he kept playing. A slow, deep melody. Not defiant. Not pleading. Just steady.

The leader noticed him. "You. Mariachi." He pointed with the barrel of his revolver. "Play something brighter."

Loren's thumb hovered a moment over the strings. Then he stopped. "I think you've taken enough," he said quietly. He stood and leaned the guitar against the stool. Silence spread through the room like a stain.

The outlaw grinned, his smile thin and wolfish. "You think so?" He stepped closer. Close enough that Loren could smell the mezcal on his breath.

The challenge came without ceremony. No speech. No threat. Just the scrape of leather as hands went to steel.

Five guns half drawn. Four never cleared leather.

Loren moved like desert wind—no flourish, no wasted breath. The room exploded with the sound of thunder in close quarters. Tables shattered. Glass burst. A woman screamed. When the smoke lifted, four bodies sprawled across the dirt floor, crimson pooling beneath them.

The fifth man—young and maybe twenty—was still alive. A bullet had torn through his gut. He crawled, dragging himself through the dirt, fingers groping for the revolver that had skittered across the floor. He was crying. *"Por favor... por favor..."*

The room held its breath.

Loren walked over and stamped his boot down between the man's shoulder blades. The bandit froze. For a heartbeat, something human flickered through Loren's eyes. Then it went out. He raised the gun and fired once. The gunshot rolled out into the desert. Loren listened for the echo, but none came. No one moved. No one spoke. Somewhere outside, a dog barked and fell silent again. Loren holstered the Colt like it weighed nothing at all.

He gathered what the outlaws had taken—earrings, loose coins, money pouches, a cheap wedding band bent nearly flat—and placed each item on the bar.

When it came to the last pouch—a heavy one thick with silver—he hesitated and then slipped it into his coat. It was enough to ride on... enough to condemn himself a little further. The rest he left on the bar.

The cantina owner tried to thank him. Loren shook his head. "No," he said. "Don't."

He saddled up before dawn. The sky glowed faint and ash-blue, and the desert smelled of creosote and last night's gunpowder. By morning, the townsfolk were talking about the shootout at the cantina. They said the man with the guitar and the gun had killed five scoundrels without blinking, then took half the silver away for himself. A drunk called him "El Mariachi Bandolero," and the name stuck.

As Loren rode away, people behind him whispered his name. Some with gratitude, others with fear—sometimes both in the same breath. Loren had seen that pattern enough to know how it went. He was a protector. He was an outlaw. He felt like neither. He was only a man who'd killed cold and clean to protect others... and then stole anyway.

***

The road swallowed him again. Days folded into one another. Sometimes he rode for miles without seeing another soul, the desert so wide it felt like the world had been emptied out and forgotten. On those stretches, only Solano's breathing and the creak of leather kept him company, and Loren wondered whether a man could disappear out here without ever dying.

The world passed in fragments. Monsoon rains drummed on tin rooftops in Sonora. Snow bit at his fingers in the high passes of New Mexico. He played by firelight, under saguaros, in adobe chapels, on rough plank stages sticky with beer. Everywhere he went, faces blurred into one another—bartenders wiping glasses, laughing men with bottles, women leaning close with painted lips and tired eyes, lawmen who nodded at him with wary respect instead of drawing guns.

The months that followed passed without distinction. Each little village had seemed the same—dust, music, drink, and the same restless ache that never quite loosened its hold. So, when he finally rode into Deming, it felt less like arriving somewhere new and more like circling back to a place he'd already been.

The town of Deming rose from the desert like a collection of tired bones with its clapboard fronts, crooked signs, and rails that hummed with distant freight. Loren tied Solano at the trough and watched the train whistle and fade across the basin. For a moment, he imagined boarding and letting the steel carry him somewhere he wasn't already known... then the thought slipped away like smoke and he walked inside the saloon to play.

The mayor—after Loren had finished playing—slid a drink across the bar, studying him. "You a thief or a singer?"

Loren raised the glass. "Depends on what the night calls for."

The portly man with the pointed goatee and curled mustache shook his head, half smiling. "Long as you leave my town with more music than trouble, we'll get along."

Still, most nights weighed heavy. Sometimes, while riding under a moon wide as the world, Loren thought he heard Nitis's quiet voice in the wind—"*A man must know the weight of his own shadow*"—or John shuffling cards beside him. Memories of Mateo's passion, Red's laughter, and Rebecca's tenderness—they all lingered, shadows tied to his boots. He told himself he was free—that he rode by choice now, not because the past chased him. Yet the gun at his side burned like a brand. And the guitar? It sang of things he wanted but could not name... peace, maybe, or forgiveness.

"You could choose a different kind of restless," Rebecca once whispered.

Those words circled him like coyotes in the dark, never leaving. Memories pulled on the strings of his heart while he plucked the strings of the guitar. *"Play somethin' not so sad,"* Red would say.

Nights came cold on the border, the stars sharp enough to cut. Loren warmed his hands over cookfires with men who spoke quietly about families they hadn't seen in years. He listened more than he spoke. It was easier that way. The songs carried what words could not.

In a dusty pueblo, he bought bread and sang for the barefoot children in the street. A girl no older than ten tugged at his sleeve after he played. *"Señor,"* why do your songs sound sad?"

He crouched to meet her eyes. "Because they remember things I wish I could forget." He pressed a coin into her hand. "Buy something sweet with that." Her smile followed him long after he rode away.

In small towns, he was welcomed with cheers. In larger ones, he was watched with wary eyes. His hands were quick with the strings and the steel, and the legend of "El Mariachi Bandolero" spread along the trails.

Some swore he'd lull you with a ballad, then vanish with your purse. Others said he gave away more than he ever kept. A few whispered he carried a curse—that every friend he rode with ended in the ground. Loren paid no mind to the rumors. His guitar, his gun, and his horse—Solano—were his companions now.

When the moon was bright, he played songs of a home he once had and wanted again, of brothers now gone, of women who promised tomorrow and never stayed. When the night was too quiet, he robbed the careless rich and gave to the poor, as if balancing a scale that would never be even.

And through it all, the desert shifted around him—the ironwood blossomed pink, the rains carved new arroyos, the mountains wore caps of snow then baked again under sun.

Time folded in on itself, each town another reflection of the last. Another cantina. Another laugh. Another theft. Another night alone.

Loren had become both outlaw and hero, saint and thief, singer and killer. He told himself he was better than the Rubies—that giving back absolved him somehow. But each night when the guitar's final note faded, and the silence pressed in, he knew the truth.

He was caught between the man he wanted to be and the outlaw he had become—still choosing, night after night, between fire and peace. Sometimes he listened for an answer in the wind or the moving sand. The desert said nothing back. Only silence and the endless echo of his own songs.

18

New Mexico Territory – 1884

The Jornada del Muerto lived up to its name. The trail was a dry, cracked scar on the earth—haunted by silence. Loren's horse picked its way across the sand, hooves crunching brittle stone until, by the second night, a thin ribbon of water appeared—the Rio Grande, silver under the moon. Smoke curled faintly on its bank. There, a small fire was burning. Loren narrowed his eyes. Someone was waiting.

It was her. Rebecca had found him.

She was waiting in the light of the fire, her hair falling loose across her shoulders, her eyes catching the glow like coals. She sat with her back to a mesquite tree, pistol belt at her side, and a bottle of mezcal in hand.

"You never were one to say goodbye, Loren," she said softly, tilting her head as he rode up. Loren knew she hadn't found this place by accident. She'd come for him.

He dismounted, tying Solano to a low branch. "Perhaps I never wanted to," he said slyly.

She smiled. "Fair enough. Sit. Drink."

Taking the bottle, he took a deep drink. The mezcal burned hot down his throat, bitter as regret. He sat down across from her on the trunk of a fallen tree, the fire throwing long shadows over their faces.

"It's been a long time. I've been hearing stories about you all over the territory," Rebecca said in a playful, flirty tone. "El Mariachi Bandolero, is it?"

"People talk. Sometimes the truth, sometimes lies," Loren replied coldly.

"You didn't leave the excitement behind... I know that's truth."

Loren looked at the glowing embers of the fire and watched the shadows dance within the flames. "Why'd you come looking?"

"Word is," Rebecca began, "an army payroll's moving east from Fort Bowie. Captain Elias Corbin—hard man, strict as a Jesuit. They say he's got soldiers enough to guard a fort, and gold enough to tempt the devil."

Loren wiped his mouth with the back of his hand and snorted. "That the same devil you're speaking to now?"

Her smile curved like a knife. "Don't tell me you've grown holy. You and I both know the saints don't ride with men like you."

"Why didn't you bring Mateo in on this?" Loren asked carefully. He gave a hard, probing stare at Rebecca. "Something happen to him and Red?"

Rebecca's eyes flashed. "No, nothing like that. They're alive. But when stories of a troubadour outlaw were being told all around us..." She touched her chest lightly. "It stirred something in me." She looked longingly at Loren. Her eyes searching for tenderness in him. "I told them I was going to find you. I haven't seen either one of them in a while."

"I see." Loren stood up, paced the fire, then sank down next to her. Her nearness was a monsoon storm. Her words were heat he knew could scorch.

"One of my friends was at Fort Bowie recently... visiting with some soldiers. I ran into her in Lordsburg. She overheard talk about the payroll transport. There isn't time to get Mateo and Red involved. And why split the gold, anyway?" She placed a hand on his leg and gently squeezed. "Just think of it, Loren—you and me. No one else. There won't be many soldiers... it'll look like a patrol. We ride in, take Corbin when he camps, and vanish before dawn. With the money from this robbery, you could buy a house in Sonora. Land. Horses. Find peace."

The word hit him like a stone. *Peace.* He'd tried before. Tried to settle, tried to sing without killing. The desert never let him stay still, but the dream never faded. Maybe now....

Loren studied Rebecca's face in the firelight... the curve of her lips, the danger in her eyes. She was trouble. She was the storm. And God help him, he wanted to ride into it.

"When?" Loren asked.

"In two nights," she said, her voice almost a whisper. "Near Lordsburg. At the river bend. It seems likely he'll stop to water his horses and make camp."

"You've got this all figured then. I don't know if it'll be enough to finally walk away, but let's do it and find out," he said. He took another pull from the bottle. Still bitter.

At dusk on the second day, Loren and Rebecca lay hidden in the brush near the Gila River. The captain's column approached—six soldiers riding in a cluster and weary from the march, their horses foaming, the captain riding tall at the front. A chest was slung over a mule at the center.

"There it is," Rebecca whispered. Her hair was tucked under a worn, tan hat. Her curves under drab overalls. She looked more miner than temptress, but Loren knew better. There was danger hidden beneath those plain clothes.

Loren felt his heart hammer. His palms were damp. He had killed before, sure, but something about ambushing men in the dark soured his gut. Still, he didn't move away.

Captain Corbin called a halt, and the soldiers dismounted, filling canteens and rubbing the dust from their eyes. One poured whiskey from a flask. For a moment, it was quiet. The soldiers were focused on rest.

Rebecca glanced over at Loren. Her hand tightened on the pistol grip. "Now."

They rose from the brush, guns drawn. "Hands up!" Loren barked.

For a heartbeat, the camp froze. The soldiers stiffened, canteens halfway to their lips, eyes wide. Horses snorted, stamping nervously at the sudden change in air. The mule brayed, tugging against its tether, the chest of gold clinking faintly in the dark.

For a moment, it might have ended clean. The kind of robbery that was more show than blood. Loren wanted it to end clean.

But Captain Corbin was no fool. His hand moved quick and he reached for his revolver, the steel flashing in the firelight. Rebecca caught sight of it and shot him through the chest before he could fire. The crack of Rebecca's shot shattered the silence. Corbin staggered, chest blooming red, and collapsed backward into the dust, his eyes still wide with fury and disbelief.

The camp erupted in mayhem. The crack of the shot still echoed against the canyon walls, the horses were screaming, and the men started shouting.

One soldier lunged forward—bayonet flashing. Loren sidestepped and shot him in the leg. The man fell screaming, clutching at the wound. Another soldier bolted for the riverbank, boots pounding on the sand. Rebecca swung around calmly and shot him square between the shoulders. He fell forward, face first into the cattails and seep willow lining the water—ripples spreading out under the moon.

The rasp of leather caught Loren's ear—one of the soldiers pulling a rifle from its scabbard. Loren didn't think—only instinct. He raised his Colt and fired. The slug caught the man high in the chest before he could pull the trigger. The soldier toppled backward—the rifle clattering uselessly against the stones.

The remaining three soldiers hesitated, fear stamped across their faces. Their weapons hung loose in their hands. They looked like men who didn't want to join their comrades in the dust. They threw down their weapons, trembling.

Loren's chest heaved. His trigger finger still tense. "Back off," Loren ordered. "On your knees." They obeyed. Slowly, hands shaking, they sank to the ground. Fear etched in their faces.

Rebecca reloaded smoothly, her eyes bright with victory. She stepped over to the captain's body—her boots scraping through the dust—and tugged at the whiskey flask from his belt. She took a deep drink. "To victory," and then tossed the flask to Loren.

Loren caught it, but his eyes lingered on the dead captain. Staring at the man's blood pooling in the dirt, he took a long swig from the flask. His throat burned—not just with whiskey but with shame. He enjoyed the thrill yet hated himself for that. The war inside. Maybe this time the whiskey would wash away the lingering remorse.

Together, they tied up the three surviving soldiers and emptied the chest of coins into large saddlebags on Rebecca's horse. They were heavy—perhaps too heavy for one mount alone, but it didn't matter. They were rich now, richer than any outlaw had a right to be.

As they rode away from the river, saddlebags bulging with coins, Rebecca laughed. Her voice rang wild and echoed in the night. Loren tried to join her, but the sound caught in his throat. There would be no song tonight.

They camped a few miles away under the shadow of a lone saguaro. The bags of money sat between them, gleaming faintly when the firelight caught the edges of a coin peeking out. Rebecca leaned back against her saddle, her hair spilling loose across her shoulders. She looked at Loren like a woman looks at a man she owns. "We did it. Simple. You and me, just like I said. Here's your piece. You can walk away from this life once and for all."

Loren sat opposite her, turning the whiskey flask in his hands. "Peace," he echoed. His voice was quiet, but

there was something raw underneath. "You ever won-
der if it's worth it?" he asked.

She raised an eyebrow. "What's that supposed to
mean?"

"Every man we kill, every coin and greenback we
steal—it don't come free. One day the desert will take
its price. And it always seems to take more than it gives."

Her eyes went cold. "Then walk away now. Be done
with this life."

He sighed. "I don't know. I'm not sure I could. I
want the quiet but I can't leave the excitement. Would
you settle down?" He searched her eyes—the embers
of fire glowing within them. He could not discern if it
was the reflection of the flames or something burning
deeper inside her.

Rebecca stared into the fire for a long while before
she spoke. "I tried once," she said softly. "To be still. To
belong to a place... to a man." She laughed—not from
humor, but out of defense. "Turns out I'm more steel
trap than wedding ring. I sprung shut on the both of
us."

Loren waited, but she said no more and he did not
press—he already knew the shape of regret when he
heard it. He put the flask on the ground and looked up

at the full moon. "I'm thinking Mateo deserves a cut of this. Red too. The Rubies have been family to us. Family should get theirs."

Rebecca sneered, "Family? Family is a noose, Loren. I had one and it nearly choked the life from me. This"—she tapped the saddlebags—"this is freedom."

Loren looked down, unsure. He wanted to believe her. Wanted to believe peace could come at the end of a pistol. The fire cracked, sending sparks toward the sky. One drifted close enough to land on his boot and die there, a tiny ember gone out in the dust—just another small, quiet death.

He was still lost in thought when he heard the *click*. The unmistakable sound of a revolver's hammer drawn back. Slowly, he looked up. Rebecca had her pistol leveled at him. The brim from her hat cast a shadow over her face. Darkness, where Loren had once seen only beauty.

"Sorry, Loren. It's the only way," she said softly, tenderly. The glow of fire now vacant from her eyes.

Are those tears in her eyes or an echo of the night sky?

The shot rang out.

Pain tore through his side, hot and blinding. He fell backward into the dust, his vision swimming. Through the haze, he saw Rebecca load the bags onto Solano and then climb onto her mount.

She didn't look back. The sound of the horses' hooves faded into the night, leaving Loren with the whiskey, the wound, and the solitude.

19

Arizona Territory – 1884

The desert was merciless.

Loren staggered alone through cactus flats and sand washes, clutching his bleeding side. Rebecca's bullet had torn a groove just below his ribs—deep enough to cripple, not enough to kill. He had managed to slow the bleeding by tearing the sleeve off his shirt, but he needed proper medical attention. He was miles from any town or village and his horse was gone. The desert had a way of making sure a man suffered before it claimed him.

Each step sent fire through his body. The whiskey flask he carried was nearly empty, and the sun had burned his lips raw. His mustang had been taken. Now it was just him and the endless sweep of Sonoran waste-land.

By the second day, his mind began to wander. He heard voices—his mother's sweet Cajun lullabies, Mateo's booming laugh around the fire, the first time he saw her and the words she whispered in his ear that night. *That heart of yours might not survive this desert.*

He stumbled across a rocky rise and froze. In the distance stood the skeleton of an old homestead. Its stone walls sagged, the roof half caved, and the chimney leaned precariously against the sky.

Loren muttered a prayer he hadn't spoken in years. He dragged himself toward it, each step slower than the last. Coming down the rocky slope, he stumbled along the loose rocks and fell into a cluster of ironwood trees and lavender.

As he trudged closer to the house, Loren could make out the remnants of the split-rail fence that once comprised the perimeter. A crumbling well stood inside the fence. He made his way over and knelt beside it. *Perhaps some salvation after all,* he thought and used the bucket to retrieve the last moisture from the ground, splashing water over his mouth. It was stale and bitter, but wet.

At last, he reached an opening in one of the walls and crawled inside. The house smelled of dust and old stone. Ravens scattered from the rafters when he entered, their cries harsh and mocking to Loren's weary mind.

He collapsed near an overturned table, staring up at a silhouetted cross made by the collapsing ceiling beams.

His thoughts drifted again. He remembered Sundays in Tubac when Padre Romero had preached under the open sky. He remembered Rebecca singing rough but strong in the Rubies' camp, her voice like smoke and honey. He remembered the quiet widow María and her kindness. What had Nitis once said? *The desert always collects on the debt owed.*

His memories were slipping further away with every drop of blood. The desert had spared him... for now. But Loren knew it was waiting.

Laying half conscious on the dirt floor, he glanced around the room searching for anything that might be of use. The house looked like it was bracing against the wind, with slumped adobe walls and roof beams jutting out like broken ribs. Sand had already begun to reclaim the floor. The whole place looked tired... like it had given up long ago.

Loren was drifting in and out of reverie. Lost between the world of what was and what could have been. Shadows danced across the cracked plaster walls, shaping ghosts of the past—Nitis taking aim with his bow, John with his two revolvers, and Rebecca's smile. He saw the ghost of himself too—a younger man with a guitar slung over his shoulder, blood not yet on his hands.

Then came the sound, faint but unmistakable—the clink of metal, the muffled snort of horses, and the soft rustle of boots through gravel. It snapped him back from his memories.

The crumbled door burst open. Shadows filled the threshold, long and hard-edged against the light of the morning. Two soldiers entered the run-down house, rifles at the ready. Behind them came a third—an officer. He was tall with sharp features and gray eyes that cut like a knife. "Well, well," Harlan said, his voice cool and crisp. "The infamous singing outlaw, bleeding out in a run-down shack. Poetic, in a way. I'm Lieutenant Charles Harlan of Fort Bowie."

Standing behind Harlan's left shoulder was a brute of a man. Squat and ruthless, his face carried a twisting scar across the cheek. Loren instantly recognized the cruel jaw—*the miner from the payroll robbery near Fort McDowell!* "Sergeant Rourke, secure the thief."

Rourke spat on the floor. "I've been waitin' a long time for this. Let's hang him right here, Lieutenant. Save Tombstone the trouble."

A younger soldier lingered off to the side. He looked to be barely eighteen, with freckles across his nose and rifle shaking in his hands. He looked at Loren and couldn't quite hide the fear—or maybe pity—in his eyes. "Private Mills, assist the sergeant," Harlan coolly ordered.

Loren pushed himself upright, hand hovering near his pistol. "You'll have to earn it, boys."

Harlan raised a brow, but his voice remained even. "You're half dead already. Don't be a fool. Lay down your gun and you'll see another sunrise."

Loren smiled faintly. Then he drew his pistol. The first shot thundered inside the old house. It tore into Rourke's shoulder. He roared in pain as he staggered back and fell to the floor.

Harlan quickly, instinctively, backed out of the entrance, taking cover against the wall. The remaining soldiers in the courtyard opened fire on the small house. Bullets smashed into the stone walls, sparks flying.

Private Mills—still inside—took cover behind a small table along the opposite wall and pointed his rifle at Loren.

Loren ducked behind a small bookcase that had fallen over next to the crumbling hearth, pain ripping through his side. He fired again—this time at Mills. The shot was deafening in the narrow room.

From outside, a volley of shots shredded into the house, shattering what was left of the window frames. Bullets slammed into the plaster, and dust filled the air. A bullet from a soldier in the courtyard punched through a gaping hole in the wall and tore a strip from Loren's sleeve. Another pierced into the hearth behind him. Outside, Harlan barked orders. "Hold your fire! I want him alive!"

Loren knelt by the hearth, his revolver spitting flame. He saw Sergeant Rourke struggle to his feet. Loren reloaded the cylinder of his Colt and got on a knee. The ruthless soldier bellowed, blood running down his arm. He charged at Loren with his bayonet fixed, fury twisting his face. Loren rolled aside and fired point-blank—the bullet burrowed into Rourke's gut. The sergeant roared, swinging the rifle like a club. The blow nearly knocked Loren to the ground, stars bursting in his vision. Rage igniting him, Loren spun, clutching his revolver, and fired again until his gun clicked empty.

"Out of bullets now, ain'tcha, outlaw?"

Loren didn't hesitate and sprang forward, charging through the smoke. He met Rourke in the middle of the room. The two men tussled, each landing blows upon the other. A stout punch to his scarred cheek caused Rourke to lose his balance. He fell hard onto a large splinter of wood from a broken chair, blood soaking his uniform. "You're done, outlaw," Rourke snarled as his head drooped forward and his body went limp.

Loren stared at the man's body. "You first," Loren said coldly. His chest was heaving from exhaustion, his hands were slick with blood—his and Rourke's both.

Private Mills was still frozen, rifle aimed but trembling. Loren met his eyes across the room. "Go on, kid," Loren rasped. "Take your shot. End it clean." Mills's jaw tightened. One squeeze of the trigger would end it. He lowered his weapon.

Before Loren could move again, the butt of a rifle smashed across his temple, sending him sprawling to the floor. Lieutenant Harlan stood over him, calm and precise. "Enough," Harlan said. "We'll take him alive. Let the judge hang him proper."

Loren tasted blood. He tried to rise, but his limbs refused. The world swam. Boots thundered inside. Soldiers swarmed around him, rifles leveled. Hands dragged him up. Shackles clamped around his wrists, biting into the skin. "Look what he did to Rourke. We should just kill him, sir," a soldier declared as they dragged Loren across the courtyard.

"Stand down," Harlan snapped. "The governor wants an example. The Troubadour Outlaw will hang from the gallows and swing in the plaza. The people will see that justice still breathes in this territory. They will see what becomes of bandits."

Loren said nothing. Harlan's words washed over him. The soldiers shoved Loren forward. He groaned and winced from the injuries. He found it difficult to walk. His boots scraped across the gravel, leaving dark smears of blood. He glanced back once at the collapsing house. Its roof timbers forming a crude cross—like some forgotten saint watching a sinner's final walk.

***

By sunset they were marching south, the desert stretching endless and cruel under the darkening sky.

Chains rattled at Loren's wrists—the iron heavy as the guilt also bound to him. Private Mills walked near him, rifle slung over his shoulder, stealing glances at the outlaw when he thought no one was looking. The kid could have killed him. He could have killed the kid. The truth of it sat heavy between them. Loren met his eyes once, then looked away. After a long silence, he spoke to the young soldier. "You ever kill a man, boy?" he asked without raising his head.

Mills swallowed. "No, sir."

"Don't," Loren said. "Once you do, he walks beside you... every night."

The young soldier said nothing.

Hours passed, the sky grew darker, the road ahead turned black. Loren lifted his head and looked as the sun slipped down below the horizon. He thought of Rebecca's face in the moonlight, of Mateo's words about loyalty, of his guitar.

Maybe this was the end he'd been riding toward all along. He whispered to himself, so low only he could hear. "Maybe I wanted them to catch me. Maybe peace ain't somethin' a man like me deserves." The wind carried his words away, scattering them across the desert.

The road to Tombstone stretched ahead, and with every step Loren felt the gallows rope tighten in his mind.

The army convoy moved slow through the high desert, a thin line of men and horses cutting across the land like an old scar. The sun rose hard behind them, burning through the morning haze, while the Dragoon Mountains shimmered like ghosts to the west.

Loren walked in the center of the troops. Like so many of the riches he plundered in the past, he was secured to the saddle of a riding soldier by a rope looped through his chained wrists. His hands were swollen, the skin rubbed raw. The wound on his side had reopened during the march, seeping through the bandage in thin red lines. Each step sent a fresh bolt of pain up his ribs, but he didn't show it.

He'd been on the trail for days, maybe more—he'd lost count. The world had narrowed to the rhythm of hooves, the clink of canteens, the dry rasp of the wind. They crossed arroyos where the water had long since fled, passed cottonwoods stripped bare by drought, skirted old homesteads where windmills still turned out of habit. Every so often they passed a cross by the roadside, the marker of some forgotten soul swallowed by the desert. Loren tipped his head in quiet respect each time.

At night, the soldiers made camp beneath the cold blaze of stars. They'd light a small fire, eat jerky and hardtack, and talk in low voices about wives in El Paso or ranches they planned to start once their enlistments ended. They never spoke to Loren unless they had to—except for Private Mills. The boy would sit near him sometimes, rifle across his knees, pretending not to care. But Loren could see the unease in his eyes. "You lookin' to talk?" Loren asked one evening as the fire cracked low.

Mills hesitated. "Just wondering, I guess.... What makes a man like you turn outlaw?"

Loren smiled faintly, eyes reflecting the flames. "Same thing that makes a preacher drink or a sheriff steal. The world doesn't always give a man a fair shake. Sometimes you take what peace you can find—even if it's the wrong kind."

Mills frowned. "You sound like you regret it."

"I regret what it cost," Loren said softly. "Men I called brothers. Women I loved. The songs I never got to finish." He looked out across the desert where the wind stirred the brush. "But I can't say I didn't live."

The boy said nothing after that.

The next morning, they broke camp early. The road turned south, tracing the edge of the San Pedro River. Vultures circled high overhead, their shadows gliding across the sand. By midday, a faint line appeared on the horizon—a town, shimmering in the heat. Tombstone. Harlan rode up beside Loren, reins taut, voice clipped. "Enjoy the view. You'll only see it once."

Loren's mouth curved into a dry smile. "If they hang me in the plaza, I'll see it from higher up than you." The lieutenant scowled and spurred his horse ahead.

The sun sank slow that day, bleeding red over the horizon. The shadows of the riders stretched long across the ground. That night they made camp for the last time before reaching town. The soldiers kept their distance, but Mills approached again, hesitant. He held something in his hand—a small, battered guitar. "Found it in the supply wagon," he said quietly. "Belonged to one of the boys from the fort. Figured... maybe you'd want it. Least for tonight."

Loren stared at the instrument. His throat tightened. "You sure Harlan won't mind?"

The young soldier shrugged. "He'll sleep through it."

Loren took it carefully, running his thumb across the strings. They were out of tune, one half snapped, but the sound that rose was soft and clean. The desert seemed to hush around it. He began to play, slow and gentle. A tune that drifted somewhere between a lullaby and a farewell. The soldiers listened in silence, heads bowed, as the notes wove through the campfire smoke. When he finished, no one spoke. Mills nodded once and took back the guitar. "Guess they weren't lying," he said quietly. "You really can make a man forget the world for a while."

Loren looked up at the stars—limitless and cold. "Only for a while," he said.

That night, lying beneath a soldier's blanket, Loren dreamed of the churchyard outside of Tubac, of Red laughing under the bell tower, of Rebecca's hair catching the light of dawn. He dreamed of a garden by a river, green and alive, untouched by blood or dust.

When he woke, the sky was pale and empty.

The march resumed at sunrise. The sound of chains followed him like music—a slow, steady rhythm marking the final miles of a song nearly finished.

20

Arizona Territory – 1884

Word traveled the way it always did in the territory—faster than trains, faster than telegraphs. It rode in on mule wagons and drifted through saloons with the cigar smoke. By the time the soldiers marched Loren Ardoin into Tombstone, it felt like half the county already knew the outlaw with the guitar had finally been caught.

Some called him a bandit. Some called him a hero. Most had a story to tell. A ranch hand swore Loren once played through the night so a dying man wouldn't be alone. A miner claimed he robbed him clean, then slipped half the gold back into his pocket. Mothers said he sang lullabies softer than church bells. Widows said he left shadows at their doors. And every tale ended the same way—they caught El Mariachi Bandolero at last.

So, the people came. And to Loren, it seemed they weren't here to see if he would hang, but how a legend did.

The noon sun burned white over Tombstone, flattening every shadow. Heat shimmered on the dusty boards of Allen Street. The smell of lard and sweat mingled with horse dung and gun oil. A brass band from Fort Huachuca had come up for the occasion, their instruments gleaming.

The square outside the county courthouse baked under the noon sun. A crowd had gathered—miners in sweat-stained shirts, shopkeepers, women shading their eyes with bonnets, gamblers in velvet coats. Dust swirled with the footsteps of hundreds gathered to see justice—or vengeance, depending on who you asked. Vendors sold tamales and mezcal from carts, their shouts mixing with the clamor. Children perched like hawks on nearby rooftops to gain a better view—their eyes wide.

At the center stood the gallows—a rough wooden frame, rope dangling like a serpent. The hangman, a heavyset man with a gut full of beer and a face baked leather-brown by the sun, tested the knot with practiced hands. His eyes were hard as the desert stones—like a man untroubled by the lives his work took. He nodded with satisfaction at his handiwork.

Lieutenant Harlan stood near the steps, crisp in his uniform, his gray eyes sharp as the iron on Loren's wrists. "Let's have order," he barked. "The people came for justice, not a circus." The crowd didn't listen.

The soldiers brought Loren out the side door of the jailhouse, shackles rattling, wrists still bruised. He moved slow and steady. His shirt was stiff with dried blood, but he no longer winced with every step. His gunshot wound had been tended to. "Can't have our bandit die before we hang him," they stated.

Loren was paraded through the crowd of onlookers. His face was bruised but he was unbroken. He looked up as he reached the foot of the steps leading to the scaffold platform—a man not seeking forgiveness, but final understanding.

The crowd's murmur rose to a roar. "That's the bandit from Tubac!" a shopkeeper shouted, spitting at Loren's boots.

"I heard he gave away his loot to the poor in Sonora and other parts of the territory," a gambler countered.

"If you ask me, he's more honest than half the politicians in the county."

A woman spat into the dust. "Those donations won't bring back my husband!"

An old, balding, pastor crossed himself. "May God have mercy on his soul."

A mother with two young children clinging to her dress raised her fist. "He's a thief and a murderer! Swing him high!"

The debate among the crowd churned like the desert wind—praise clashing with curses in Loren's ears. The noise rolled like a wave until the town marshal fired a warning shot into the air. Silence followed, tense and trembling—the kind that made Loren's skin crawl.

On the scaffold, Loren stood with the rope brushing his shoulder. The crowd pressed in, a sea of faces that looked like a mixture of fascination and contempt. His eyes wandered over the crowd. He saw people he'd known fleetingly—gamblers he'd drunk with, women he'd charmed with a song, a prospector he'd once cheated at cards. Looking for comfort, he found none.

The hangman eyed him coldly. "Got any last words, outlaw?" he asked, tightening the knot at the back of Loren's neck.

He looked at the hangman—his hands steady, his eyes dull with the repetition of his trade. Loren forced a smile, though sweat trickled down his neck. "How much they pay you for this?" he asked.

The large man frowned. "A hangman's fee. Enough to feed my family." He slipped the noose around Loren's neck. The hemp was coarse, smelling faintly of creosote and death.

"I got more," Loren said, lowering his voice. "There's money hidden—a lot of it. You let me slip away, it's yours."

He chuckled, humorless. "Every man with a noose on his neck swears he's sittin' on treasure." He tugged the rope, testing its weight. "You'll swing like the rest."

Loren's jaw tightened. For once, it seemed his words had no sway. He closed his eyes for a breath and thought of the mission—Nitis's wisdom, John patiently teaching him to shoot, and Red's booming laugh by the fire. He could almost hear his mother's lullaby from a lifetime ago. He opened his eyes and wondered—not for the first time—whether peace waited on the other side of a rope. Whether the songs would finally fall silent.

As the noose settled around his neck, Loren scanned the crowd again. He saw the widow María—who had once given him bread and gardening advice. The marshal from Mesilla was in the crowd too. *The song or the gun. You can't carry both forever.* Those words echoed in his head.

Just then, something caught his attention at the edge of the crowd—a flash of golden hair beneath a dark shawl. Rebecca. *What was she doing here?* Her eyes locked on him, wet with unshed tears. Her lips moved soundlessly—*hold on.*

Then he saw it—Mateo shifting through the crowd. And Red! He was leaning heavily against the base of the scaffold stair rail, eyes scanning the soldiers instead of the crowd. Something was coming.

The hangman raised his large hand and placed it on the lever that would open the trap door. The crowd hushed.

Then Rebecca let out a sudden wail, staggering forward toward the scaffold as though she was possessed by a spirit. "Please... don't! He's innocent!" Her cry sharp and desperate. Two soldiers standing near the base of the gallows moved to restrain her. One soldier bent down to catch her arm.

The hangman momentarily paused and watched the scene. It was brief, but in that instant Red quickly leaped up the stairs—moving faster than a man his size should—and lunged at a soldier on the platform. He slammed into him, ripping the revolver from his hand.

Mateo rushed onto the platform from the other side. His hand slipped into the sash tied around his waist. Steel flashed. He moved past the hangman and pressed a small blade—slim and sharp—into Loren's palm. "Now, *hermano!*" Mateo hissed.

The hangman took his hand off the lever and reached for Loren. It was too late—the rope snapped. Loren's desperate cut had set him free and in the same motion he slashed the giant man across the arm and knocked him to the floorboards.

Mateo drew a pistol from his sash and fired twice in the air. The crowd erupted into chaos. "Gun!" someone screamed. The band scattered—brass horns clattering into the dust. Onlookers hastily dispersed. Vendor stalls overturned. More gunfire cracked through the air like lightning splitting dry wood. Its smoke curling in the hot air.

Mateo darted across the platform. His pistol barking, a second blade flashing in his other hand. He effortlessly spun about like a dancer performing on a stage as the bullets chewed into the platform beams around him. His laugh rose above the chaos—a wild, reckless sound.

Red, holding the revolver he had taken from the stunned soldier, fired down toward where the crowd had been only moments before—dropping two soldiers before they could raise their rifles.

Loren tore free of the scaffold, jumped past the hangman, and vaulted down the steps. His boots hit the dirt hard. He picked up a soldier's revolver that had fallen to the ground and fired into the crowd of uniforms, bullets snapping off adobe walls. Another soldier lunged at him with a bayonet. Loren fired point-blank, sending the man spinning into the dust.

Both Red and Mateo rushed down the platform steps next to Loren. "To the back alley!" Red shouted. Rebecca broke loose from her captors and ran toward them, skirt torn, hair flying. Loren grabbed her, pulling her behind him. For a heartbeat they locked eyes... there was no time for words—only the sharp ache of everything they'd never be. Red and Mateo laid down fire toward the advancing soldiers. They plunged into the mayhem—soldiers shouting, townsfolk screaming, a tamale cart ablaze behind them.

Loren fired as he ran, covering their retreat toward a narrow passage between adobe walls. Bullets snapped past, shattering plaster and wood. Rebecca stumbled, but Loren caught her hand, pulling her along. "Keep running!" he gasped.

Amid the pandemonium, Loren's thoughts flickered like lightning. He should have felt triumph—freedom clawed from the gallows's teeth. Instead, all he felt was the heavy weight of another chain—loyalty owed to the men beside him. "This is no freedom," he muttered, cutting down another soldier who lunged with a bayonet. "It's just another debt owed."

Mateo heard him, blood on his sleeve, grin wide. "Better a debt than death, *hermano*!" he shouted back—his voice wild with adrenaline.

They fought their way clear, toward a side street, the sound of rifles and screams echoing behind them. The Rubies vanished into the alley onto waiting horses, leaving the plaza—and the thick, acrid smell of gunpowder and blood—behind. Smoke coiled above the gallows like a ghost unwilling to leave. The rope swung gently in the desert wind, as if waiting for the neck it never got.

21

Arizona Territory – 1884

The desert opened wide before them—a sea of pale sand and shadowed rock stretching to the ends of creation. The sun bled red across the horizon, casting long bars of light across the Chiricahua Mountains. The peaks glowing like embers in a fire. The horses panted, their hooves drumming a steady, hollow rhythm echoing off the mountain walls.

Mateo rode ahead, tireless and sure, pistol slung low on his thigh. His outline cut sharp against the dying light. Loren thought he looked like a man still chasing purpose. Red followed behind, coughing through the dust, muttering curses at every jolt of the saddle but refusing to slow.

Loren and Rebecca were riding together, a slight distance back from Red. Rebecca was pressed close, her arms encircled around Loren's waist. Her hands felt the wound where she had shot him. Her cheek brushed against the back of his neck. She said nothing, but Loren felt the weight of her silence. He wasn't sure if the silence was full of memory, guilt... or something like hope. It was heavier than any saddlebag of gold.

As the stars began to blink awake, they made camp in the low hills, where mesquite and ocotillo clawed out of dry ground. A fire crackled, smoke curling into the cool night. Coyotes called in the distance—lonely, restless, familiar.

Mateo uncorked a flask of whiskey and raised it high. "To the rope we left swingin' behind us!" he toasted. Then passed it around with a grin.

Red laughed. It was a deep, ragged sound that ended in a cough. Blood spattered his sleeve. He muttered, "Ain't every day a man gets born again."

Loren stared into the fire as the words settled over him. *Born again.* He supposed that was true enough. He'd stood with the rope at his neck and felt the world narrowing to a single point, and then—gunfire, chaos, the hand of a friend hauling him back from the dark. A man didn't walk away from that unchanged. And yet....

The iron shackles might have fallen from his wrists, but his soul still felt their weight. The outlaw life still clung to him like dust after a long ride. Guns at his side. Men willing to kill for him. Blood spilled in his name, or because of it. Freedom wasn't in the running—not really. Freedom, he was beginning to understand, was a quieter thing than gun smoke and legend.

The flask passed to Loren. He took a deep drink, feeling the burn settle in his ribs, then passed the flask to Rebecca. She didn't take it. Her gaze remained fixed on him—steady and unreadable—as she opened her mouth to speak, but Loren cut her off before any words came out. His voice was low and hard. "Back near Lordsburg... you shot me and ran off with the take. Left me to bleed in the desert."

The fire popped between them. Rebecca flinched. Her lips parted, but she didn't deny it. Instead, she leaned closer, voice trembling. "I wasn't trying to kill you," she said softly. "I knew you'd never leave this life willingly. I lost someone before who wouldn't walk away. I couldn't let it happen to you too." Her lips trembled. "I thought if I hurt you bad enough, maybe you'd stop." Regret dripped from every word. "When I heard you'd been caught..." She shook her head. "I knew I couldn't let it end like that."

Loren studied her in the firelight. This was the woman who had once kissed him behind a cantina in Hermosillo, laughed as she slipped cards from her sleeve at the poker tables in Las Cruces, whispered promises in the dark, and vanished into the desert with his trust in her saddlebag. He saw every lie, every truth, in the shifting light of the flames. "Where exactly is my peace?" he asked quietly.

Her gaze didn't waver. "Your share's waiting. Buried south of Alamo Hueco. I can take you..."

Loren raised his hand, stopping her. She didn't understand that he wasn't talking about the stolen army payroll. For a long time, neither spoke. The wind picked up, scattering ash and sparks. Somewhere out in the darkness, an owl called—one long, mournful note.

At dawn, they rode again, following the arroyos and dry riverbeds. Every mile took them farther from soldiers and gallows, deeper into outlaw country. The days blurred together—pale sun, red rock, silence. Sometimes Loren thought he saw shapes in the distance—the ghosts of Nitis and John riding in the heat mirage. At night, he'd wake to the crackle of the fire and Rebecca humming softly beside him, her voice haunting and fragile.

Loren could feel the impending weight of choice pressing on him. Rebecca cut out the gang on the last heist and she double-crossed him, but she came back and aided in his escape. He was unable to determine if she was ready to put the outlaw life behind her. If they had been playing cards, she would've had a perfect poker face.

On the third night, she led them to a lone mesquite tree twisted by wind and time. Beneath it, half buried in dust, lay a guitar—his guitar—the strings dulled with sand. She brushed the dirt away and propped it against the tree trunk. Beneath the instrument was a saddlebag. She dug it out herself, nails breaking, breath ragged. Inside, wrapped in oilcloth, lay stacks of gold coins—the stolen payroll.

Loren knelt beside her and picked up a coin. He turned it in his fingers then ran his hands over the rest of the coins in the bag. They shimmered in the light of the moon. Enough money for a new life. A quiet place far from hangmen and gun smoke.

Mateo and Red watched from a few paces off, their faces unreadable. Mateo crossed his arms and finally broke the silence. "You can walk away now, *hermano*. Take the gold and ride south. Away from this life and from us. It's okay."

Loren looked up and met his eyes, the moonlight cutting across his face. "I owe you both for saving me from the hangman. Take what's yours. I don't aim to owe a man, or the rope, again."

Mateo's grin widened. "*Gracias, hermano*, but no. This is your peace. I will find mine someday."

Red chuckled. "I'm sure mine's in a bottle, not that bag, anyway."

A satisfying calm swept over Loren as he stood up to embrace his brothers. The three men stood in silence a moment. The kind of silence that settles at the end of a long trail—full of things that'll never be said. "But come daybreak, ride fast before I change my mind," Mateo said with a sly grin.

That night, Loren and Rebecca sat apart from the others, watching the fire slowly fade to ash. She leaned her head against his shoulder. He whispered, "Maybe we could make it work." His voice was soft. "Down in

Sonora. No one would know us. I could play. Put my guitar to work instead of my gun."

Rebecca didn't answer at first. She ran her fingertips over the battered instrument, then over Loren's hands—those same fingers, calloused by trigger and rein. He drew the guitar into his lap and brushed his thumb across the strings. A low, mournful tune filled the desert night—a tune caught somewhere between sorrow and salvation.

After a long silence she said, barely above a breath, "Every time you ride out... I think maybe that's the last time I'll see you." She swallowed. "Back near Lordsburg, I did what I always do. I tried to get ahead of the hurt before it caught up to me again." Her voice trembled, just once, then steadied. "I never meant to lose you. I just didn't know how to keep you."

Loren kept playing, his eyes fixed on the fire's last glow. "You think a man like me can ever be done with blood?" he asked.

Rebecca lifted her head and met his gaze. "I hope so."

It was not the answer Loren wanted, but he understood that she could never follow him toward peace...

and he would not find peace staying with her. His heart ached with that truth.

The final notes of the guitar slipped into the night wind. Thin and fragile, they lingered for a time. When at last the music disappeared into the darkness, silence settled over the desert.

Neither spoke again.

At dawn, the last of the Rubies stood at the fork in the trail—west toward California, south into Mexico. The horizon flowed pale gold, promising nothing but distance.

Mateo and Red were going to ride west to California, chasing another scheme, another golden dream. Loren was headed south, toward something quieter. Mateo clasped his arm. "You'll never ride alone, *hermano*."

Loren looked faintly at Mateo. "I know."

Rebecca lingered where the roads divided, her horse restless beneath her. She looked longingly at Loren—eyes pleading—waiting for the invitation to join him, waiting for forgiveness. Loren met her gaze, then looked away. The silence between them said enough. Her invitation wouldn't come.

After a long moment, her lips parted—as if she might speak—but no words came. Some things are beyond mending with breath alone. She turned her horse east—toward a future neither of them spoke about.

Loren only nodded at her, then turned his horse south. The road ahead stretched endlessly—a promise, a curse, a kind of peace. He strummed a soft chord on his guitar as the sun rose over the mountains. The sound drifted on the wind—half prayer, half farewell.

And then Loren Ardoin—the outlaw, the troubadour, the man who'd danced with death more times than the saints could count—rode into the horizon. Behind him, the outlaw's life—loud, violent, relentless. Ahead, for the first time in a long time, lay a road that belonged to him.

As he quietly trotted toward a life of peace, Loren thought of the last time he made this choice and the words Nitis spoke to him, "*The desert always collects on the debt owed. Most men do not get to choose how they pay it.*"

A slight grin formed on Loren's hardened face. *I will choose.*

It wasn't a clean ending, but it was his.

EPILOGUE

Sonora, Mexico – 1891

Years later, in a smoky cantina in Hermosillo, Mateo leaned back in his chair, boots crossed on the table. The railroad had reached the city by then, and the plaza outside buzzed with mule carts and gossip brought down from the border. The stubble on his face had gone gray at the edges, and his left hand stayed stiff from an old bullet wound. Red was gone now, buried somewhere in the desert near a mountain of manzanita shrubs—or so the story went—in a place where the coyotes never seemed to quiet.

The *cantinero*—a short, pudgy, balding man—poured him another mezcal from a cloudy bottle. "You hear the tune last night?" he asked, jerking his chin toward the corner. "A gringo. Plays guitar like the devil, sings like an angel."

Mateo's eyes narrowed slightly. "What kind of song?"

The barkeep shrugged. "Low and lonesome. The kind that keeps a man at the table longer than he planned. He lives in the mountains nearby. Rides down when the weather's good. Plays a few songs, has a drink. Doesn't ask for coin. Just leaves."

The dice rattled. Men laughed. A soldier cursed at a losing hand. A ceiling fan squeaked on its tired bearings.

For a long moment, Mateo said nothing. Then he smiled—slow, sharp, and touched with sadness—and raised his glass in a quiet toast to the memory of an old friend.

The "El Mariachi Bandolero," he murmured. "*Hermano*... you found your peace after all."

The mezcal burned his throat, but he didn't cough. He motioned for another drink.

Outside, an evening wind scraped along the cantina walls, carrying dust from the Sonoran hills. Mateo thought—or maybe only imagined—that a faint ribbon of music rode with it. A tune worn thin by distance and years, still traveling the desert like the last prayer of a restless soul.

www.ingramcontent.com/pod-product-compliance
Lightning Source LLC
Chambersburg PA
CBHW061436150726
47987CB00001B/233